WARRIOR'S SONG

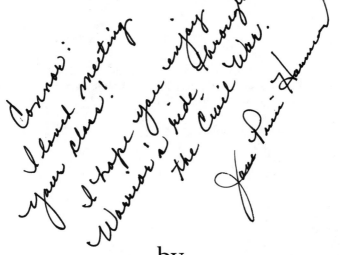

by
Jane Price Harmon

Photography by Pansy Brandt Winters

First published by Dog Ear Publishing
4010 W. 86th Street, Ste H
Indianapolis, IN 46268
www.dogearpublishing.net

ISBN: 978-1-4575-2523-0

This book is printed on acid-free paper.

This book is a work of Fiction. Places, events, and situations in this book are purely
Fictional and any resemblance to actual persons, living or dead, is coincidental.

Printed in the United States of America

To:

Mikell, Maude and Paxton van der Heijden

CHAPTER 1

*T*he moonlight made Warrior's flaxen mane shine as if lit by fireflies. Sayre gripped the lead rope with a determination that had come from her Irish grandmother, whose auburn hair and freckles she had also inherited. Warrior nickered softly and Sayre kissed his nose.

"It'll be all right. You'll see. But right now, the Yankees are coming and I have to hide you. You must be safe. You just must because Papa will be so glad to see you. She paused and unwillingly added, "When or if he comes home once this horrible war is over. You know what a big smile he has when he's happy." That image floated in her mind and she fell silent, trying to muster her own smile, but fear gripped her. "We were so happy before all this began. Oh, Warrior, I hope he hasn't been hurt. We may not know where he is, but if you and Freeman and I are here when he walks down that road and sees the farm, he'll smile for sure."

The horse and girl were moving through the trees, heading for a dim light in the distance. Warrior whinnied, his ears pointed forward, his keen senses telling him that the familiar figure of Freeman was ahead. Ducking under the last branch, Sayre broke into a full run, her bright chestnut horse easily keeping up with her every step.

"Here we are. Everything ready?" she called.

"Yes'm," Freeman said as he emerged from the shadows. "The hay and grain, water too. All there. Enough for a week

1

at least. We'll put him up just fine. No way those Yankees are gonna find this horse! We just tuck him in tonight and wait for old Mr. Sherman. It's sure lucky Mr. Overby come by to warn us. I got our chickens and hogs stowed way up in the hills with the Overby flocks. We'll find out when that army is coming through and then we'll decide what we do next. Wonder what other folks are doin'."

"I don't know. Hiding things and animals, like we are. Do you think Lee's army's nearby? Maybe there'll be a huge battle. Surely General Lee wouldn't let the Yankees come through Georgia without putting up a fight!"

"Sure think he's around somewhere. Wish I knowed where. Then we'd all feel safe, even our four-footed young un here." They approached a cleft in the hillside. "Well, here it is."

Sayre dropped the rope. Warrior was trained to stand— her father had seen to that—but this time the young horse moved back just a bit, peering at the deeply cut hillside, his ears pitched forward, his instincts telling him to mistrust the blackness inside.

"This is your home for a while, Warrior. Don't worry. One of us will come to check on you every day, if we can." She hurried on, as much for her own sake as for the horse's. "You'll have plenty of food and water, but not much freedom, I'm afraid. We just have to keep you safe."

Sayre opened the gate Freeman had built at the entrance to the hillside stall, and walked in. It was cool and dark, with straw on the ground. Covered bales of hay were piled outside next to a barrel which contained the feed. Freeman had secured the grain with an elaborately designed top meant to confuse and repel any critters looking for a free meal. Feed and water buckets hung in two recesses dug into the side of the hill and shored up with wooden supports. It was a perfect hideout for her most precious possession, her most ardent companion.

She looked around, touched the sides of the earthen stall and went back out to bring Warrior inside. This was the moment she had been dreading, leaving him here alone, but it would be only for a short time, just long enough for her and Freeman to plan what to do next in this most dangerous time.

Gently she picked up the rope and led the horse into the cave. This time he didn't hesitate, always confident with her. Sayre took his head in her hands and kissed his velvet muzzle.

She looked deep into his dark eyes and whispered, "You're okay. Just wait for me or Freeman to come tomorrow. We'll watch for the soldiers. There's plenty of food and water and the gate will keep out any animal big enough to hurt you. Maybe a cardinal will keep watch over you. You know that's our angel in disguise, at least that's what Papa says. Remember when he told us he'd send feathers to let us know he was thinking of us while he's away?"

And he had kept his word, for Sayre had found any number of feathers, each of them carefully collected during the two years he'd been gone. They were stored in a box on the table by her bed. Each one was precious to her, a talisman.

She hurried outside, shut the gate, locked it, and stepped back. Now she would be totally alone, except for Freeman. Her father was fighting somewhere with General Lee, her mother was in the freshly dug grave on the hill overlooking the creek, and now Warrior was hidden in this isolated part of the farm.

"C'mon, Miss Sayre," Freeman said," We've done all we can. Ain't nothing more, 'cept wait for them villains to come."

Sayre turned. Warrior nickered. She could hear him begin to pace. He was not accustomed to being confined.

The pasture near the farmhouse was his home; the stream that ran through it and the trees that provided the shade from the hot Georgia sun, his playground. She could not look back. Freeman was right. All that was left to do, the worst part, was to wait and see what General Sherman would do after his monstrous victory in Atlanta.

CHAPTER 2

$\mathcal{T}$he next morning, Sayre was up at first light. She made a quick breakfast of eggs and bacon and biscuits left over from last night's supper, carefully scanned the road for any signs of Sherman's soldiers, then headed up into the hills to see Warrior. Approaching his makeshift stall, she whistled the sound she had perfected which always made him fly from wherever he was to where she held a carrot, his favorite treat. She smiled, for her distinct whistle was the only one to which Warrior would instantly respond. When other people called his name, the horse would come at his own speed—after stopping to nibble grass, gaze at the sky, or rub the blaze on his nose against his leg. Warrior ignored even her father's attempts at whistling. Outwardly, Papa had been annoyed that Sayre had bested him in this, but she knew he was secretly pleased.

Immediately Warrior's head appeared from within the cave and he whinnied a grateful greeting. Sayre fed him two carrots and put the halter over his head, attached the lead rope, and led him outside to a pasture, a small piece of flat land nestled between the gently rolling hills. The grass was thinning with the approach of winter, but was still plentiful. She unbuckled the rope and Warrior lowered his head to eat. Thank goodness her part of Georgia had had abundant rain this year. The grass that stretched out before her was luxuriously green. Sayre sat down and savored the smell of Warrior's body, his huge head grazing close to her.

"Did you spend a sleepless night like I did? Well, enjoy a little freedom, and I'll be back this afternoon if no Yankees show up or Freeman'll come up to give you more water and hug your neck. I thought I'd just sit with you for a bit and let you eat to your heart's content. Then I'll head back down. Freeman and I have work to do in the garden."

Sayre paused, got up and paced a few steps. The enormity of her situation—being left, first by her father and then by her mother, and now facing the threat of invaders—was overwhelming.

When she continued talking, her voice was soft, distant as she spoke to the trees. "You know, Warrior, it's already November. November 20, 1864, to be exact. Can't believe it's been almost two years since Papa left. If I'd been a boy, I bet I could've gone too. Even though I was only twelve. Papa said he'd leave us here so you and I could protect each other and Mother. I know he misses you. He always bragged about you being so special!"

Her mood shifted as she imitated her father's hearty voice when he brought Warrior from Kentucky and introduced him to Sayre and her mother. "'This is my Saddlebred from Kentucky! Yessir, the horse Kentucky made. He's fast and beautiful under saddle, and very intelligent.' "Did you hear that Warrior? Fast and beautiful under saddle and very intelligent.' "I know he was afraid someone would steal you if he took you into the war. I also think he didn't want you to get hurt, but he didn't say so. I reckon he figured it was best to do the fighting without either you or me."

Sayre walked to the horse, took his head in her hands and spoke directly to him. "I just wish we'd hear something, Warrior. Did Papa get my letter about Mother and the fever and how terribly lonely we are now?"

There was a long silence before Sayre spoke again. "I know I shouldn't be thinking sad thoughts. Remember how Papa always said you can't change what happens? You can only choose how to react, and I should be brave." She let her hands fall as she turned and sat down. Warrior rested his face on her shoulder, and she automatically stroked it, her fingers moving over the taut skin.

She looked at the sky, at the sun slowly beginning to command the day. "Yes, that's what he said, I'm pretty sure: 'You can only choose how to react.' That's probably somewhere in one of those Shakespeare plays he loves so much. You know, Warrior, sometimes I just plain forget what Papa said or how he said it or even how his voice sounds. Anyway, you just keep eating and I'll sit and watch you. You can tell me how happy you are not to have to plow or haul rocks today. You're a man of leisure for a few days. I guess I can call you a man now that you're six and fully grown! I'd sure love to hop on your back and race down the road to see if the Yankees are near, but that would be a bad idea, I know. You could be a goner for sure if I did that." Sayre moved her hand over his neck and felt the warmth of his skin and the powerful muscles beneath his skin.

Visiting Warrior like this was so foreign to her. She was used to seeing him throughout the day. Whenever she glanced toward his pasture, she could catch a glimpse of him. Sometimes he'd have his head over the fence watching her working in the garden, the house or barn. Then she would talk to him, always looking forward to the time when, her chores finished, she could leap onto his back with or without a saddle and head into the woods or down the road to the Overby plantation.

Sayre checked the progress of the sun and knew she had to leave. She reluctantly picked up the rope and led Warrior back into his stall, curried him and gave him a few more treats before locking the gate.

Burdened by how alone she felt, she walked down the steep hill to the log farmhouse, now silent without the animals. The image of her father's departure, something she hadn't dwelled on for a long time, wouldn't leave her thoughts. The last time she'd seen him, he'd had a bedroll on his back and was headed to meet other men from the towns of Gordon and Griswoldville. She had watched until he disappeared over the hill, only turning once to smile and wave. In her mind, she had played and replayed that image for months afterward, but it had become cloudy with too many days filtering in and out. Now, with more fear wrapped around her life, the image had returned clearer than before. She wanted Papa to come home, to sit and talk with her, to take away the fear and make sure Warrior would be safe.

At the farm, Sayre looked for Freeman and found him repairing the axle on their tired wagon. She sat down beside him. "Since you're pretty calm, I'm going to guess Mr. Overby hasn't come with any news."

"Guess you're right," he replied. "How's our man? Holding up? Did you tell him we're gonna charge him for rations since he's not working? I know he's handsome and charming, but we've gotta draw the line somewhere."

Sayre smiled at the image of Warrior. "He's fine. I let him eat some grass, and we talked like we always do. I told him you'd be up later. I'll straighten up the house and then we'll head for the garden. Maybe some hard work will make the time go faster. I've never been very good at waiting."

"Nope, but there's plenty of other things you can be proud of, and Mr. Howard would be the first to name them if he wasn't off fighting."

"I know. The first thing he'd say to me at the beginning of each day was, 'Sayre, good morning, and it is a good morning because you're my daughter.'

She turned, brushed a tear from her eye, picked up a bucket, and walked to the well to fill it. Then she headed inside the farmhouse to sweep the floor and begin mopping. She and Freeman were always challenging each other to see who had the cleaner home. Sayre tried to claim a disadvantage since her house was bigger, but Freeman wouldn't relent. His cabin was, indeed, small and roughhewn—one room with a bed, table, a couple of kerosene lamps, a fireplace, and a rocking chair—but it was his, and he was a free man. Sayre's father had signed the documents before leaving for the war. Those precious papers, now tucked inside a box on the table near the rocker, proclaimed to all the world that this man, once a slave brought to this country as a boy from Africa and now a man of forty two, belonged to no one.

Freeman's first major decision as a freed man had been to stay on to help with the work and to watch over Sayre and her mother when Mr. Howard left. Sayre's father had explained that he wasn't fighting for slavery. That, in his opinion, was a dying institution. But he was a Southerner. He respected General Lee and didn't like men in Washington telling Georgia what to do, so he had to fight. Freeman had accepted that.

When she finished cleaning, Sayre stood back to admire her work. The four rooms shone. Her mother would have been proud! Sayre had been a diligent daughter, duly learning how to clean, sew and knit, how to grow and cook her food, how to make soap and candles. Teaching her to ride had been her father's greatest gift, she thought, even above reading and writing. Nothing could compare to riding, to feel her body and Warrior's locked together in a walk, a trot, a canter, or a full gallop. And the places you could go! Just the two of you, through the woods, over a stream, far up into the hills where a gray fox could cross your path or a red- tailed hawk could glide for miles on the air currents above you!

Satisfied with her housework, Sayre grabbed a hoe and headed for the garden, but the sound of hoofbeats on the road made her stop. She turned, her heart beating fast, and recognized their friend, Mr. Overby, galloping toward her. He reined in and dismounted.

"Freeman around, Sayre?"

"Yes, sir. Are you here about the Yankees? Have you seen them?"

"Haven't seen them, but Confederate scouts from Wheeler's cavalry came by a few hours ago. Let's go talk to Freeman."

They didn't have to go far. Freeman was running from the garden, shovel in his hand.

"Mr. Overby. The Yankees?" he called.

"Not yet, but they're on their way. Some of Wheeler's men rode up to the house last night. They were tired and hungry, but they told us what they knew of the Yankees' movements. We shared one of Dorothy's finest Georgia suppers, including my favorites, turnip greens and cornbread. Come to think of it, her sweet potatoes weren't bad either. Anyway, the men had a good night's sleep and a hot breakfast, then left early this morning. They were moving fast. Seems the Confederate Army is trying to pull together as many troops as possible to stop Sherman."

Sayre and Freeman exchanged glances. They knew how Mr. Overby loved to eat. And to talk.

"Now here's what I know: Sherman's got about 60,000 troops, and he can move through Georgia fast because they're traveling light. They're young, too, a lot of them under eighteen, but they're already battle-seasoned, especially after Atlanta. I don't know what we can muster, but it sure isn't that many troops, not even close. Most of our men, like your father, Sayre, are away serving with other regiments so there's nobody much left to fight. When the Blue Coats left Atlanta—let me see if I can get this right—they were split into two wings, the northern army under Slocum, the southern one, which is what we have to worry about, under Howard with Kilpatrick's cavalry protecting their infantry."

The man noticed his young neighbor's expression and interrupted his own story. "Yes, Sayre, I'm afraid there's a Yankee general walking around with your surname!"

Then Mr. Overby was back to business. "There's about sixty, maybe eighty, miles between these two armies. They're burning houses, killing or stealing livestock, and tearing up any rail lines they come across. Apparently, they heat the rails until they're red hot and twist them into spirals or wrap them around trees. The armies were not given many supplies and were told to live off the land, and I do mean live off it! Georgia's got plenty of food and they aim to take it and leave us to starve. But your livestock and mine are well hidden. How about Warrior? I know he's what you really care about."

"Freeman and I hollowed out a stall for him in a hillside over near Shiney Woods. He should be fine. So what do we do now?"

"We wait and pray. Remember when your father told you about what happened when the city of Rome was sacked by barbarians? I've heard him tell that story more than once. Well, that's what we have here, a huge bunch of barbarians, in my opinion, and they're intent on doing a lot of damage to bring the South to its knees. You two need to come back with me. Dorothy would welcome the company. Leave everything here. You're fourteen, Sayre. The Yankee Army is full of hot-blooded young men. I'm very worried." The big man seemed to have finally run out of words.

"I know, and thank you, but Freeman and I will just have to meet what's coming head on. I guess we won't be getting much sleep, but that's the least of our worries."

Freeman, who had been quiet, asked, "So there ain't no Southern troops coming to our rescue?"

"Only Wheeler's cavalry is operating around here, picking at Kilpatrick's men. Our generals did have a huge meeting at Macon after Sherman swept through there. Let me see if I can remember: Hardee, Beauregard, somebody named Smith, oh, and Richard Taylor, son of old President Zachary Taylor. They were all there, as well as some Georgia politicians, but it appears it's too late to save Georgia. Now, General Phillips did put up a good fight outside Griswoldville, but the Federals had already burned most of the houses in town, along with the factories and the depot. The men at the house last night said our lads got slaughtered by the Yankees' repeating rifles, a poor commander, and their inexperience. They were brave, as always. Now a lot are dead."

Freeman turned and walked a few feet away before turning back to speak. "Sounds bad. I reckon I'll be safe since I'm a negro. The Yankees are fighting for me. Probably, they'll want to carry me off to fight with them." A smile flickered on his face, "Or to cook for 'em. But, Miss Sayre, you should leave. Mr. Overby"s right. A young lady's not safe in this situation."

Sayre knew that what the men suggested was sensible, but hiding with the Overbys was not what she wanted to do. Sensing that she had to speak up or lose the chance to make her own decisions, she replied, "I'm sad for Georgia, for my father, and I'm so very scared for all of us, but I won't leave Warrior or the house or Freeman. I guess the three of us will face whatever comes to our door."

Freeman was silent, but Mr. Overby started to protest.

Sayre added hurriedly, "But, how's this: I'll do it as a boy, just like in *As You Like It* and *The Merchant of Venice*. I'll cut my hair, and I have some of Papa's clothes. I can make them fit. Please understand. I just have to look after what little of mine is left. I'll gladly be a boy for awhile."

Mr. Overby walked to her and put his arm around her shoulder. "Are you sure, Sayre?"

She nodded. "I'm as sure about this as anything I've ever done. I'm my papa's daughter!"

Chapter 3

That night, Sayre again hiked up to visit Warrior. She was afraid of the Yankees. Her heart pounded at the thought of a foreign army in her beloved South. Tonight the hair on the back of her neck stood up at the night sounds in the woods. She couldn't remember all the names Mr. Overby had attached to the army units that were coming through Georgia or where they were going or where they had been. He had given her a lot of information, but he was like that. He loved facts, dates and names, but they were now all a confusing blur. It didn't matter who was in charge of the troops. The danger was real. The names were unimportant. Yankees were nearby, swarming through her beloved homeland.

It was calming to muck Warrior's stall, bring him water from the branch nearby and fresh hay from the spot where Freeman had stored it. Sayre brushed her horse, combed his mane and tail, picked his hooves, and talked to him as she always did. Reluctantly she returned to the farmhouse to set about the task of disguising herself as a boy to help her survive.

Sayre pulled out a pair of scissors from the drawer in her mother's sewing box and cut her hair just below her ears, just as she'd seen her mother trim her father's rich, dark hair. When she had finished, she scooped the fallen deep, auburn strands into her hand and rubbed them

14

across her face, relishing the color and texture because it was exactly like her mother's.

She chose a pair of her father's gray pants and cut the legs shorter. Then she pulled a faded blue shirt and heavy white undershirt from the same drawer, the drawer that held all the clothes he'd left behind. She slowly put her arms into the shirts, savoring his half-forgotten smell. Pulling on the pants, she laughed out loud. They were definitely too large, so she cut a piece of rope and belted in the waist, then trimmed the legs more to fit her 5 foot 4 inch height. She looked at her image in the mirror over the dresser. The shirts disguised her small breasts. For now she was thankful she had her father's lean build, not the shapely figure of her mother. Sayre had always wanted her curves when she'd thought of becoming a woman, but not having them now might protect her. She decided to pitch her voice a bit lower and tried different sounds until she found one that was easy to use and seemed natural. She picked up the book containing all of Shakespeare's plays, randomly found a page and read it aloud using her new voice. She continued reading until the sound came naturally.

When she finished her disguise, she went to the pasture beside the house and buried her hair under a bush near the edge of the woods. Then she returned to the farmhouse and surprisingly fell soundly asleep, not waking until there was a loud banging on her door. She bolted up, checked her face in the mirror, threw on the shirts, pants, boots and an old hat of her father's, and ran to the door. Opening it, she was face to face with five Union soldiers, rifles cocked.

"Who lives here?" the tallest soldier demanded.

"I do," she responded in her newly invented voice.

"Son, where's your ma, your pa?"

"My mother is dead. My papa's off fighting with General Lee."

"Anybody else around?"

"Yes, sir. Freeman. He's a freed slave. Papa freed him before he left, but Freeman stayed on to help me and my mother. Then she died. Typhoid fever."

"You know who we are?"

"I guess you're Yankees fighting for Sherman."

"We are, and if you're lyin' to us, there's gonna be hell to pay. Where's your meat cellar? You're gonna provide us with as much food as we can carry, son. Don't care nothin' 'bout your troubles. Now step out here. We need to take a look inside. You, Wayne, find the meat cellar, find this freed man and see what you can scrounge up. Move. We gotta travel fifteen miles today."

Sayre sat on the steps while the soldiers invaded her house. Freeman joined her. The muscles in his face were tightly drawn, his brow furrowed more than usual.

"You all right, Sayre? They're taking all the meat and most of the vegetables. Looked through my ole cabin, but nothing much there interested them."

"I'm okay. Not much in the house to interest them either, thank goodness."

The tall soldier came out of the farmhouse with two of his men. He whistled for the others who were at the cellar behind Freeman's cabin. They soon reappeared, slung the meat over the backs of their horses, put the vegetables in huge cloth saddlebags, and mounted up.

"I'm Lieutenant Meyers. I'll leave one of my men here to guard the property so the troops that are coming won't hurt you. Mr. Overby told us about you. Our General Howard is using the Overby plantation for his headquarters tonight and tomorrow. The Overbys said you don't have no livestock because the Confederates already stole everything. By the way, who's the reader? You got quite a collection of books in there, even Shakespeare."

"My father, and he taught me. Shakespeare is his favorite."

"Can't beat Shakespeare. Heard he's the best. Anyway, our orders are to give you some protection. The boys can get carried away sometimes. They're young, headstrong, and it's been a long, hard campaign. But we'll win. That's a given now."

Sayre stiffened, but said nothing. She put her clenched hands behind her back and thought of her father.

Lt. Meyers's voice brought her back to reality. "We'll be on our way. You and Freeman should be fine. I'll leave Lt. Daniel with you. You should see the front of the army any time now."

The four soldiers turned their horses, laden with Sayre and Freeman's food, and galloped up the road. Sayre caught herself glaring after them and turned coldly to the remaining Yankee.

Noticing how uncomfortable the boy looked, for he did appear quite young, she spoke, "You want to sit on the porch?"

"Nope. I'll just stay near the road. Got some buddies in the other outfits, and I wanna see them go by. Haven't seen them since we left Atlanta on November fifteenth. That's a short time for the distance we've covered."

"Well," Sayre took a deep, steadying breath, "I guess I'll draw some water, get a couple of dippers, and have it all here if the Bluecoats want it. Don't mind helping, even if they are on the wrong side."

She added silently to herself, "And I can keep an eye on them. Plus, if they think we're friendly, they may not go looking for anything else we may have hidden."

When the bucket and cups were in place beside the road, she sat down on the front step and rested her head in her hands, feeling very small and quite alone. She didn't know how long she'd sat there when she heard a huge rumbling and looked up to see the road filled with men, most in blue, most with a poncho slung over their shoulders, a haversack, and a tin cup hanging at their waist. Each had a rifle and a cartridge box. A few were on horseback, others riding in wagons, but most were walking. All were moving quickly, laughing, talking loudly as if they were on a church picnic rather than a march to destroy her beloved South.

Sayre moved to the bucket and filled canteens when they were held out to her. Freeman kept replenishing the water in the bucket. Occasionally, their young guard would hail someone he knew, but generally the army moved rapidly by: men, horses, then cattle and pigs, and at the very end, black men, women, and children walking or riding on mules or in wagons. Once Sayre was startled to see a young soldier ride back and yell at the blacks.

"You're going too slow! Either pick up the pace or go back. We're headin' for Savannah, and we have to be there in a month, and no broken-down passel of negroes is gonna stop us. So get moving. Now."

The blacks quickened their pace, evidently not choosing to go back to their masters and the only life they had known. Freeman watched this, jaws tightening. He went to a few of the wagons to talk to the men in rushed whispers.

The wagons with the wounded came next. Their pace was much slower. There were at least twenty wagons pulled by mules and filled with men, boys really, looking young and vulnerable. Some lay flat, most sat upright. Their wounds were swathed in bandages of all descriptions.

From the end of this surreal procession came the sound of a fiddle, and Sayre's heart jumped. The tune was so familiar, one her father had played many times at Mr. Overby's dances at the plantation. That fiddle was still in the house, leaning against Papa's chair. He had left it with Sayre so she could play it for her mother. Years ago, he had taught her to play just as he had taught her to ride. She hadn't touched the fiddle since her mother's death, but knew the tune. "To Laxley Green," swirled through her head, and she found her foot keeping time.

When the wagon with the young musician passed by, Sayre clapped her hands and called to him, "Sounds great, even if you are a Yankee. Where'd you learn to pull a bow like that?"

The young man beamed. "Kentucky."

"Kentucky? Why're you fighting for the North? You're on the wrong side."

"Don't look that way, son. We're headin' through Georgia to whip ol' Lee good, and I'm gonna play the whole way. My music will get these sorry-lookin' fellas back up and fightin' again."

"I guess your music might do that, but they'll have to recover fast before General Lee gives them the whipping of their lives. Here's some water so you can play longer," she said, and handed him a dipper.

He drank it and thanked her, then picked up the fiddle and began plucking out "Shall We Gather at the River." Sayre stood back and watched the last of the army move up the road, the strains of that old familiar tune echoing back through the woods even when they were out of sight.

Sayre put down the bucket and ladle and walked to Lt. Daniel and spoke quietly, "Lieutenant, I was wondering if I could shine up your horse. I'm pretty good at currying. My father used to have a horse and he showed me how." Then she added, "He rode off with him to join Lee. It looks like your mount could use some attention. I have a few brushes in the barn. It won't take long, and I'd like to thank you for being here."

"That's mighty nice of you and he sure could use the attention. Trace is a good horse, actually the best. Been with me four years through some mighty tough battles. Brought him from my farm in Illinois. Have at him, son. And thanks."

Sayre ran to the barn, glad to be able to again feel the warmth of a horse under her hands. Trace was smaller than Warrior. His coat was rich and black, accented by a flowing black mane and tail. He was muscled from use in the war. He stood quietly as she brushed him, picked his hooves, and combed his mane and tail, all the while talking to him. His ears flickered in response, for he knew from her touch that these were experienced hands. When Sayre had finished, she stood back to admire the animal.

Hoofbeats on the road from Mr. Overby's plantation pulled her from her thoughts of the horse, the war, and the men who were fighting on both sides. A lone rider on a large bay reined in near her.

The young man called, "Lt. Daniel, let's move. We're needed at the front of the column. Nothing nor nobody's behind me. You've done your job here. Let's go. These folks are safe. Right, son?"

Sayre found herself staring at him—his black hair under his hat, his deep gray eyes—and she forgot what he'd asked.

"Son, I'm taking Lt. Daniel with me. Is the black man around or did he join the others behind the troops?"

"He...he's here," she stammered. "Freeman's here. We're fine. And thank you."

Lt. Daniel mounted his newly gleaming horse, turned to the young captain, and said, "Let's go, sir. If Sherman needs us, he's got us! Thank you, son, for the water and for cleaning up my horse. Trace just about shines."

The lieutenant reached down and patted his horse's neck. The small gesture showed Sayre how much he admired, even loved, this animal that was carrying him through the war.

Sayre was quiet for a minute, and then said timidly, "Trace is beautiful. Good solid lines. Strong too."

Lt. Daniel tilted his hat to her, placed it back on his head, and grabbed the reins. Both men tapped the sides of their mounts, and the two horses leapt forward to carry their riders down the road and out of sight, leaving a silence behind that filled the valley and engulfed the small farm.

Sayre was still watching the empty road when Freeman came up beside her and spoke, "I'm gonna see how Warrior's doing. Haven't been up today. He'll be thinkin' we've abandoned him, and I got a lot to tell 'im. You stay here. If any more Bluecoats come by, tell them I've gone looking for a hog that got loose. I'll be gone about two hours. I'll let Warrior out to graze a bit. I think you'll be okay."

The reality of Yankees in Georgia was as plain as the hoofprints in the dirt at her feet. Sayre knew that she and Freeman had to maintain the illusion of an ordinary routine about the farm. If anyone were watching, it would make more sense for Freeman to be out in the fields while she stayed to keep an eye on the house. Still, it felt like a hardship to stay home instead of dashing off to see Warrior.

Sayre sighed and spoke with more ease than she felt. "You know I'll be fine with you looking after Warrior. I guess we should leave him hidden for a while until we're sure they've gone. Lt. Daniel said that Sherman's moving very quickly to Savannah. After Savannah, he said they were going through South Carolina, which is Sherman's main target, and then on to North Carolina. Seems that since South Carolina was the first state to leave the Union, he wants to teach them a good lesson. That's a long march they've got ahead of them and I do hope they run into a lot of trouble on the way.

Surely our troops won't let them destroy Georgia and the Carolinas."

"There's a lot of trouble to go around for sure. For everyone. But it's a good idea to leave our boy hidden a while longer. Don't know who's gonna be prowling around."

"Hug him for me, Freeman. I'll go up in a few days."

Sayre turned and walked to the small white clapboard house, stepped onto the porch, and opened the door. It was cool inside, and she could scarcely believe that Yankees had been here, inside her home. She walked from room to room reclaiming it as her own. The furniture was rough, but somehow her mother had softened everything. White cotton curtains fluttered at every window. There were quilts made by her grandmother and her mother, even one that Sayre had pieced, a tablecloth she and her mother had crocheted, and, of course, her father's books, each worn from the touch of a hand that had worked hard in the fields. She ran a finger over every one, then stopped to kiss the last and dearest one, *The Complete Works of Shakespeare*, a volume of ivory pages sheathed in leather. She took it from the shelf and sat down in the rocker. Sayre simply held the book and laid her other hand on the top of the box that held the feathers. Tears filled her eyes, and she cried because she was afraid.

Chapter 4

The next three days passed uneventfully. No more Yankees came down the road. Mr. Overby rode over to say that the officers who stayed with him were "such perfect gentlemen that he'd almost forgotten they were Yankees." Freeman visited Warrior at dawn each day to assure the horse that he was not forgotten. The war, this terrible upheaval that had changed their lives completely, seemed far away.

When Sayre was in the garden turning the soil over for the next year's crops, she did think of the captain with the lovely gray eyes, then wondered why anybody's eyes should be so important to her right now.

"But," she thought, "he seemed kind and so did Lieutenant Daniel."

She couldn't shake the impression of how young they both looked, too young to be officers. But she knew the Confederate army was also recruiting younger and younger men as the war wore on. At least that was what Mr. Overby said. She wondered how old the captain was.

"Twenty-two, perhaps?" Her voice was her only company. "Silly thoughts for a silly girl dressed as a boy."

Soon she would be able to shed these clothes, let her hair grow back, and return to the life she knew, keeping everything ready for the time when her papa would come home. She could picture it so vividly, dashing into his arms and breathing in his comforting scent. Then they would race to Warrior's pasture to see a horse as beautiful as the day her father left. The fields and farmhouse, too, would be orderly and well-tended. Papa would be so proud of her.

"Sayre," he had said the night before he left, "take care of your mother. You and she are quite a team, and there's no one more competent than you. We never had a son. In fact, you were all we ever wanted. I've taught you to be independent, and your mother has taught you to be compassionate. That's a winning combination. Never forget that. And never forget how much I love you and how proud I am of you."

This morning she would finally go to see Warrior. She could hardly wait to hold his head in her hands, look into his deep, dark, intelligent eyes, brush him and feed him carrots. Mr. and Mrs. Overby were coming by for supper, but she would have all afternoon to cook. The meal would be simple: vegetables and cornbread. That was all that was left, all that Freeman had been able to hide in a hole he'd dug in the woods near the pasture. Sayre knew she was lucky to have even that. She had heard the soldiers say that Sherman wanted nothing left behind, "If their families are starving and there ain't no slaves to do the work on the farms, those Confederate Johnnies will want to race home. That'll mean surrender, and that's what we're aiming for."

Sayre finished her chores, stored the tools in the shed, and went to find Freeman. He was in the woods across from the cabin, where he'd just felled a small tree and was chopping it into firewood for the winter.

"I'm going to check on Warrior. I'll be gone a couple of hours. Do you think that'll be okay?"

"Yep. That army's moving fast. We'll see Mr. Overby tonight, and he'll have plenty of news. I'll work here, and then I've got some mending to do at the barn. Four boards on one side rotted out. You go on. Our boy'll want to see you."

"Should I give him a kiss from you?"

Freeman laughed. "Plant several for me, Miss Sayre. Tell him we'll throw him a party when he comes back."

Sayre grinned as she ran across the road, past the house and Freeman's cabin and into the woods that led up to the hills behind the farm. About halfway up, she slowed, taking in the stillness around her and contemplating their good fortune. The Yankees were gone. She smiled, looked down, and spotted a feather half hidden in the leaves. She stopped to pick it up, a blue jay feather, a sign from her father that he was watching over them and all was well. She tucked it inside her pocket and kept climbing toward Warrior.

When she was near his hiding place, she whistled her special whistle and he whinnied back! It took her barely a minute to reach him and begin caressing his neck. She threw the halter and lead rope over his head, and trotted with him to the pasture near his hiding place. She sang to him and told him about the Yankees, Lt. Daniel, and the handsome captain with the gray eyes. She assured Warrior that the captain's bay and Lt. Daniel's black stallion, although quite beautiful, were nothing compared to a chestnut Saddlebred with a flaxen mane and tail!

Sayre sat on the grass as Warrior ate. She sang and let herself talk to her father, then to her mother, all the while reveling in the fact that her beloved horse was nearby. Maybe tonight, after Mr. and Mrs. Overby left, she would pick up the fiddle and play a tune. That would be the perfect end to a perfect day.

Finally, she said, "Well, Warrior, I've been here a little longer than I thought. Let's go back. I'll muck the stall and get fresh water and hay for you. You'll be here for another week maybe, just to be safe. Freeman thinks all the Yankees have gone on to Savannah. Maybe General Lee will be there waiting for them. We'll see what Mr. Overby thinks tonight."

Together, the girl and the horse moved from the pasture to the stall where he stood obediently outside as she cleaned the area and made it ready for another day. Sayre was almost finished when she heard a twig snap, and her heart stopped.

"Freeman?" she asked as she stepped outside and ran to grab Warrior's lead rope. Her horse's ears were pitched forward, twitching in response to a foreign presence in the shadows of the trees. Then his nostrils flared and he nickered softly. Seconds later, Sayre heard a rifle cock and she leaned her head into Warrior's, instantly realizing that the worst of dangers had found her.

"Saddlebred, ain't he?" a hard voice said from the shadows. "Time to hand 'im over to ole Joe, the best bummer in the Union Army. I can forage with the best and find anythin' you Southerners have hidden from us, goats, chickens, pigs, silver, even peach brandy! Knew somethin' was up here. Didn't realize it would be this prize. My captain'll be mighty grateful to have a horse this fine. You gonna tell me his name? At least fifteen hands, I'd say. Five or six years old?"

"His name is Southern Warrior." Sayre's voice was low, measured. "He is fifteen-two hands and is six years old. My father bought him in Lexington, Kentucky, three years ago. You know your horses. Are you going to shoot me?"

"Son, I only want the horse. And, yes, I do know my horses. I'm from Tennessee. Mother was a Cherokee. Worked around Saddlebreds a lot when I was a farmhand. Sorry, but that's about all the time I have fer conversation. Just hand 'im over now. You go sit in that nice stall, shut the door and don't come out for an hour. If I hear or see ya,"- his voice was now low and cruel -"I'll shoot 'im, understand? My men are down below holding that Negro. Keep your head, son, and your Warrior'll be all right. Go on. Inside." When she didn't move, he barked, "Now!"

The last word was a command, uttered so severely that Sayre started moving backward, her hand not leaving Warrior's body, her farewell lingering on every inch of him until there was no more of his soft hair under her hand.

"Goodbye, my Southern Warrior," she whispered. "Go with Joe. I'll be fine. Be the bravest horse, and everyday I'll think of you and pray you'll be safe. You'll come home, I promise."

She backed into the stall, shut the gate, and watched as the bummer took the rope and led Warrior through the woods and down the hill. The mottled sunlight splashed across her horse's back and tail as it swished through the trees. He whinnied only once. When she could hear only the rhythm of his hooves descending toward the cabin, she took two steps backward and fell to the soft earth. His smell was everywhere. It was cool and quiet. On the earthen wall nearest her she saw a patch of hair from his tail or mane. She stood up, collected it, and held onto it tightly as she sat down again. Then she put her head in her hands and wept uncontrollably, her wails echoing from the enclosure and through the trees.

CHAPTER 5

Sayre didn't know how long she had stayed in this place, which was now so special to her, a place surrounded with memories and the scent of Warrior-her beloved Warrior-her glorious horse. The sun was overhead, warm for November. Her heart ached. Everyone was gone: her father, her mother, and now Warrior. All she had known, a life filled with love, music, security had been blown away by the war, the fever, and the words, "Just hand 'im over." Only Freeman remained. That thought made her stand. Where was he? Was he alive, hurt? The man had said there were others at the house and cabin. What did he call them? Bummers"?

Sayre threw open the gate and began to run, to scream, "No! No! No!" She raced down the hill and then froze. She smelled smoke. Now she began blindly stumbling, yelling, sobbing. When she cleared the woods, she saw flames devouring her home. Freeman was standing nearby and there were tears streaming down his face. He turned when she shouted his name. Blood was oozing from a cut on his forehead. She ran to him and he caught her in his arms.

"Warrior!" she screamed.

"I know, Miss Sayre."

"Are you all right?" she choked out through her sobs.

"Yes'm. Just a disagreement between me and the Blue-coats. Looks like they won for now."

28

Sayre dropped to the ground, sobs heaving from her body. Her beloved Warrior was gone. She wanted to die. What was left? What was she to do?

Freeman walked to the well and brought up a bucket of water, then went inside his cabin for two soft rags. He wet both, handed one cool cloth to Sayre, and began cleaning his wound with the other.

Sayre ran the cloth over her face. Her breath was coming in short waves. She rose and went to Freeman. "Let me see what they did to you. What did they hit you with?"

"A rifle butt. They just wanted to feel tough, I reckon. Thought they'd beat up a Negro to make themselves feel better when they decided to burn your house but not mine. Beats all. But this cut ain't half as bad as the feeling in the pit of my stomach."

Sayre rinsed the cloth in the bucket and dabbed gingerly at Freeman's wound again, wishing for a way to heal the wound inside her, but knowing that only the sight of Warrior galloping back to her could do that. She forced herself to take a deep, slow breath, but she needed to move, to run away from the pain.

Turning from Freeman, she looked at the smoldering ruins of the farmhouse. Nothing really mattered now. The ache inside, the hurt that penetrated every particle of her being, blocked any thoughts. There was nothing more. Everything was gone. She began to walk.

Without knowing it had been her intended destination, she approached her mother's grave. She sat for a few minutes and then lay her head on the mound, her tears watering the moss that had just begun to grow oh so very timidly there in the last two months. Sayre had no words to say to her mother. At other times, she had come here to gather strength or courage or ideas for how to survive in this mysterious adult world, but survival wasn't important now. She would welcome death. Life without her mother, her father, and now Warrior meant nothing.

What was the purpose? The day, so bright with promise and happiness at its beginning, creaked along now with its bitter burden of loss and disappointment. As the sun was beginning to set, Sayre sat up and watched the creek flow by below. She didn't even turn when she heard her name.

"Sayre, darling!" It was Mrs. Overby. "Oh, Sayre, I'm so sorry. I know that sounds trite, but it's all I can think of now. Andrew is with Freeman. Will you come with me back to the cabin? Oh, my precious child. Come here and let me hold you."

Sayre stood, but didn't speak. Mrs. Overby put her arm around the girl and supported her as they walked to Freeman's cabin. Inside, there was a small fire in the fireplace. Freeman and Mr. Overby were sitting on either side deep in conversation. A pot of soup was cooking and Sayre smelled cornbread.

She stood in the doorway, looking in. She blinked, trying to focus. The scene made no sense. She barely recognized where she was, who these people were. Their voices were distant.

Freeman rose and came to her. "Miss Sayre, not everything's gone. I did have one piece of good luck."

She looked at Freeman, not quite recognizing him, then turned and walked to the ruins that were once her house. Parts of it still smoldered. She stood silently. Her home was utterly destroyed.

Freeman's voice was behind her. "If you come back to my cabin, you'll see I saved a few things."

"Things," she repeated and then she slowly turned and followed him.

"There," he said pointing at his bed in the corner of the room.

On the quilt lay her father's fiddle, his book of Shakespeare, and the pictures she had drawn of Warrior last year. The small box that held all the feathers she had collected in two years was also there. She raised her head to look at Freeman. Somehow this man had saved her most precious possessions. She could not believe such kindness in this violent and brutal world. Without thinking, Sayre felt in her pocket for the bluejay feather and the bit of Warrior's hair. Her hand closed over them. She pulled them out, opened the box, and placed them gently inside arranging the clump of Warrior's hair on top. It sparkled even in the dim light of the cabin.

"Yesterday morning, after you left to see Warrior, I laid them by just in case there was mischief from any more Yankees. Hid them in the barn under some hay."

Sayre tenderly ran her fingers over the objects.

Mrs. Overby spoke softly. "Sayre, we want you to eat now. I know you aren't hungry, but I don't want you to become ill. We've lost your mother, we can't lose you! Come on. Sit down with us. Freeman and I have made a great sweet potato soup, turnip greens and cornbread. Maybe it'll make you feel a bit better."

The woman gestured to the small wooden table and Sayre sat down. Mr. Overby was uncharacteristically silent. She looked at the faces that surrounded her, only barely understanding why she was here.

When they had finished the meal, Mr. and Mrs. Overby cleared the table and Freeman washed the dishes. Sayre just sat and stared at the fire. When everything was in order, Mrs. Overby walked over to the girl and hugged her.

"Good-bye, Sayre," she whispered. "We'll check in tomorrow. We have to get back tonight. We can't leave the house and land very long, even though the slaves are there. They all chose to stay, except Billy, who joined the troops as they marched by. One Yankee even took Nellie's petticoat and wore it over his uniform as he marched down the road. She ran after him to get it back, yelling at the top of her lungs, but he pointed his gun at her and she fled back to the house crying for all she was worth. That petticoat was her prized possession! But we'll work on a new one for her."

Sayre raised her head and spoke for the first time, "Good-bye, Mrs. Overby, Mr. Ovrby and thank you. My father loved working for you. He always said you folks were good to our family."

Mr. Overby chimed in. "Your father was the best craftsman in these parts. He learned a lot from those Shakers up in Kentucky. I never walk up our cherry staircase without thinking of the pride he took in building it. No supports-it's a work of art. He meant a lot to us. Still does. As you do, Sayre."

Sayre lowered her head and her tears fell to the ground. Mrs. Overby hugged her again. And this time Sayre leaned into her, feeling the comforting fullness of her body.

When they were gone, Sayre turned to Freeman. Her voice was devoid of emotion. "I'm going up to sleep in his stall." She turned to leave, but then said, "I'll need a blanket. May I borrow one?"

"Of course," he responded and walked to a trunk near the bed. He pulled out an old quilt with a wedding ring design, then went to the fireplace and picked up a lantern, lit it and handed it to her.

"Thank you, Freeman."

She turned and started the long trek to the now abandoned stall. At the edge of the woods, she stopped and looked back at the spot where her house had stood. Warrior's pasture was on the right, the garden on the left. She looked at the barn, the woods across the road. This had always been her home, everything that she held dear had once been here.

When she reached Warrior's stall, she opened the door gently as if entering a sacred place, for it was just that to her. She walked around it touching the walls. Slowly she moved the remaining straw into a pile and lay down.

"I love you, Warrior," she said and once again tears flowed down her cheeks.

She blew out the flame in her lantern and then saw a faint light coming toward her through the woods. She sat up and was ready to run, but then she heard a familiar voice.

"Miss Sayre, don't worry. Just reckoned this was the place to watch the stars tonight. Besides, you need another blanket. Use this one. It's a mite chillier then we thought. You go to sleep. I'll just be here, thinkin'."

Sayre smiled. "Thank you, Freeman."

She took the offered blanket and lay down again. The last words she whispered before falling asleep, surrounded by the scent of her beloved horse were, "Don't worry, Warrior. I'll find you." With this, she snuggled into the hay, somehow sensing that an adventure was about to begin.

CHAPTER 6

"*M*iss Sayre?" Freeman's gentle voice woke her from a deep sleep.

"Freeman," she said as she looked around, slowly remembering why she was in a pile of hay in Warrior's hill-stall.

"Miss Sayre, it's daylight. Reckon we should go back down. I know we got things to do today."

By now she was standing, folding the blanket and quilt and brushing the hay from her clothes. "We do, Freeman. I've got to get a few things together. I'm going after Warrior." This she said as she swung open the gate to the stall. "I'll need to go to Mr. Overby's plantation to borrow his mule, Beauty, if he'll let me. Maybe you can help me pack? I won't need much really. Then I'll head down the road. When I find them, I'll just explain what Warrior means to me, and I'm sure they'll give him back. If I can find Lt. Daniel and the captain, I know they'll understand. And I can surely travel faster than a whole army, so I reckon I'll catch them easily. I shouldn't be gone longer than a week, maybe two. You stay here and do what you can to protect your cabin and the farm. Actually, you've already rescued all the valuables I have, if you can call those valuable. I'll leave them here with you."

Freeman looked at her incredulously. What was she thinking? This was not the world she knew. This was war. She was so young. Sometimes he forgot that.

"Miss Sayre. Ya can't do that. Most likely the Yankees won't give you Warrior back, and besides, ya could get killed before ya even find 'im. Child, I won't let ya do that!"

Sayre straightened, her eyes now blazing. "Child! You call me child! And you won't let me leave. You have no authority to tell me what I can or can't do. Remember who you are. You were a slave and my papa freed you! I am going after Warrior. No one can stop me, not you or the Overbys. My life has ended on this farm! I am going to find my horse!"

Freeman stared at her, then turned and walked down the hill toward his cabin, the words Sayre had hurled at him still ringing in his ears. They had hurt more than he could have imagined. Sitting in his rocking chair this morning and thinking would help put the situation into perspective: maybe he could puzzle out a workable solution, something to keep this very hardheaded child safe. He owed that to her father.

Two hours later, the door to his cabin opened slowly. "May I come in, Freeman?" Sayre asked.

"Don't mind," he said, continuing to rock.

Sayre walked in, lowered her head, and said, "I'm sorry. Those were terrible words that came rushing out of my mouth. It's just that I have to try to find him." Tears spilled from her eyes. "Please understand. He's all I have left, besides you. If you try to stop me from leaving, I'll sneak away because I'm sure I have to go. I came to ask if you would go with me to the Overbys' to see if I can borrow Beauty to hitch up to our wagon. "

" All right, Miss Sayre. I know there ain't no way I can keep ya here if ya want to leave. I know how stubborn you are."

Sayre smiled. "Point well taken."

After a meager breakfast of cold biscuits, Freeman and Sayre walked the two miles to the Overby plantation. It was not a grand house, but a typical red-brick Georgian that was large and accommodating. The family had sixteen slaves housed in four cabins built of bricks made on the property. Now that the slaves had been freed by President Lincoln, Sayre wondered how long they would continue working for Mr. Overby. She saw that some were in the field: a few plowing, others dropping seeds into the furrows. These, Mrs. Overby had said, had chosen to stay at least for now, but their world had been drastically changed.

Sayre stopped and looked around. There was little destruction, but clearly the army had camped here. The yard, once immaculately manicured, had been trampled by feet, hooves, and heavy wheels. She and Freeman stepped onto the broad front porch and knocked.

Mrs. Overby answered the door immediately, an apron covering her full skirt. Her hair, blond with streaks of gray, was tied back with a kerchief. She held a large feather duster in one hand and a cloth in the other.

For a moment, she stared at Sayre, still not accustomed to the girl's altered appearance: the baggy shirt and pants, the boots, the hat covering the cropped hair. But there was more. Sayre looked older now than her fourteen years. Her eyes held an unmistakable sadness.

Mrs. Overby summoned her voice. "My goodness. Sayre, Freeman. Come in. My husband will be so glad to see you! Andrew," she called as she moved down the hall toward the back of the house, "Sayre and Freeman are here." Then turning to her two guests she continued, "I'll just be a minute. I'll make some tea. Just stay right where you are. Or better yet, show yourselves into the library. I'll only be a moment." With that she turned and hurried toward the kitchen, which occupied a small building behind the house.

Freeman and Sayre walked into the library. Sayre glanced around her, once again taking in the beauty of the room, the shelves of magnificently bound books, the mahogany furniture, the rich carpet under her feet. As if drawn by a spirit, she turned and moved toward the hall. The cherry staircase her father had made dominated the entry, its deep red tones warming the area. She ran her fingers along the wood. He had made it as the Shakers at Pleasant Hill had taught him-no supports, freestanding. How he loved to build, to work with beautiful woods to create something lasting. The Overbys were lucky that the Yankees hadn't burned their home, and Sayre felt she shared that good fortune when she gazed at this staircase. She was still standing there, rubbing the wood, taking in its burnished smell, when Mrs. Overby appeared with a tray that held a teapot, cups, saucers and a plate of sandwiches. Andrew Overby followed closely behind.

"Well, Sayre," he said as he ushered her back into the library, "we're pleased to see you this morning. We've been worried about you and Freeman there all alone. Dorothy and I talked last night and both of us agreed we'd like it very much if the two of you came here to stay with us. There is an empty cabin in the woods for Freeman, and I could certainly use another hand on the farm. Dorothy can always use help around the house or in the kitchen. You could go back and forth to see your farm or plant a garden, but you both would be a lot safer and we wouldn't worry as much. Right, Dorothy?"

"Absolutely," Mrs. Overby replied. "Here, sit down and let me pour you both some tea and we'll try to be civilized at least for a while."

She busied herself with the teapot and, smiling perhaps too brightly, handed Sayre the first cup.

"Sayre," she said, "your hair looks very nice short. You did a masterful job of cutting it. And in your father's clothes you really can pass for a boy. I'm impressed."

"Thank you. It's hard to get used to, but I did fool the Yankees."

She glanced at Freeman, hoping he might initiate the topic that had prompted their visit. He cleared his throat.

"Mr. Overby," Freeman began. "Are all your folks stayin'? Any more of them joined Mr. Sherman?"

"No. Thank goodness. Only Billy. We're just now beginning to sort through the changes. We're trying to get enough food for the winter. Those Yankees took almost every bit we had. I'm going to get the livestock down from the hills this week. I think we're out of danger_" Here, he stopped, suddenly mindful of Sayre's losses.

"Mr. Overby," Sayre said. "we came because I'm going after Warrior. I need to catch up to them, hopefully find Lt. Daniel or that captain, and explain what Warrior means to me. They just have to understand and they'll give him back."

"Sayre, I'm afraid you can't do that," Mrs. Overby broke in. "That would make us far too anxious. It is a foolish idea and absolutely fraught with danger. I know you're upset. But that!" She rose and walked to the window. "You and Freeman must come here dear. You'll be safe with us. And don't think of it as charity. I confess I could do with the help. Our Adelaide is in Savannah with her own family and we don't see her very much, particularly now. We know the Union Army is marching to Savannah, and we are growing more concerned by the day." The strain of recent events rang through her voice. She turned to her husband. "Andrew, do something, please."

Unwilling to face down both Overbys, Sayre rose quickly and heard herself speaking with newfound purpose, "I don't know what we would do without you both, but I can't let them keep Warrior. There's nothing back home for me, and Freeman can watch over the place. I'm not afraid."

Taken aback, Andrew looked at Freeman, who was very quiet. "What do you say?"

"I was hopin'you could persuade her to wait awhile, think it over more. But, I know her pretty well. Ain't no keepin' her here if she's determined to go. The only way I can think of to keep her safe is to go with her.."

At this, Sayre wheeled around.

"No, Freeman. It's not your battle. It's mine," and her voice dropped, "And Papa's. I want Warrior home when papa walks down that road. I can do this by myself."

"You can do a lot, Miss Sayre." Freeman said. "No doubt about that, but not this, not now that the world's turned upside down and backwards. The only thing is, Mr. Overby, we need an animal to pull our wagon and we've come to see if we can borrow Beauty. Our wagon's in pretty good shape. I think it'll travel."

Mr. Overby stood and began pacing the room. Everyone was quiet.

"The danger," he said. "My God, she's a child. The danger is too great. And—," he glanced at his wife, who sat aghast on the settee, "I cannot go with you."

Freeman continued. "Of course not. They didn't take my gun. I managed to hide it. I reckon a black man can get free passage, and a white man's not much help. Might even get us shot. We'll go home today, take Beauty with us, if we can. We'll get our things together and come back tomorrow to say good-bye. Sayre'll dress as a boy; it worked when the army came by."

Mrs. Overby's pale face was now trembling. "Sayre, I know what Warrior means to you. I also know deep down you won't be happy without him. Life seems to have dealt you a very difficult hand, all of us really, but you in particular. You'll grow up too fast, Sayre. You'll see things that will change you forever, and I don't want you to know more pain."

"I'm already grown, Mrs. Overby. I've already lost a lot. I won't sit here everyday wondering what's happened to Warrior. My Mother is gone forever and I can't go find Papa, but my horse is still within reach. I will find Warrior and I'll make sure he comes back alive. We'll all come back alive."

Mr. Overby walked to the window. He stood there, hands clasped behind his back, shaking his head, looking out at the fields beyond. Then he spoke in a low voice. "I'm sorry, Sayre. I can't help you do this foolish thing. I have some responsibility to your father, and I won't be a part of a plan like this that puts you in so much danger."

"Mr. Overby,"Freeman began. "You're shore nuff right, but if you don't help us, I'm gonna have a devil of a time keepin' a watch on 'er. I know she'll go with or without us. She's already threatened that!"

Mr. Overby turned to Sayre. She met his gaze, her head held high. It was a long time before he spoke.

"Then, I suppose, it's settled," he said. "We'll drink our tea, get Beauty, and then discuss how we can help you with supplies. I managed to bury some food and I'll gladly share that with you. Thank goodness the Yankees didn't want that old mule. It's the only time being blind in one eye ever came in handy for her. However, let me reiterate that Mrs. Overby and I are very reluctant to participate in any way in what I consider a venture fraught with danger."

"Thank you, Mr. Overby," Sayre said. "I'm glad you understand and can help."

40

CHAPTER 7

The sun was just barely rising, but the wagon stood ready. Beauty was grazing in Warrior's pasture, not knowing she was about to venture into war. Mr. and Mrs. Overby had arrived early, coming to the farm intent on talking Sayre out of her quest, but Freeman had intervened, speaking to the couple as Sayre filled canteens with water. As the girl brought a quilt from Freeman's cabin and placed it on the wagon, she saw that the Overbys had begun transferring supplies from their wagon to hers, and she knew they were resigned to her departure.

Even with the addition of these neighborly gifts, the cargo was sparse. There were blankets, two bedrolls, a skillet, a coffee pot, a tin of coffee and two mugs, two forks, two knives, sugar, several rations of bacon that had been hidden at the Overby plantation, two woolen coats, and two ponchos for the rain that would soon soak the Georgia countryside. Both Sayre and Freeman had a cloth bag filled with one change of clothes and a few personal items, including scissors to keep Sayre's hair trimmed.

Freeman also had a smaller bag, which contained herbal remedies they might need. His favorite was green wormwood, but he also had some brown wormwood for fresh wounds, vinegar, catnip for fevers, oil of turpentine, sulphur, black tea and strong alcohol, plus two ounces of creosote. Any doctor in any army would have been impressed. Freeman was a wizard at healing, using skills he'd learned from Dr. Thomas, the man who bought him at the slave market in Savannah.

Freeman had been eighteen when he was taken from his tribe and shackled into the hold of a ship that had sailed from his beloved Africa to the shores of America. Blinded by the southern sun, he had struggled upward only to find himself shoved forward and sold into an uncertain and dangerous future in this new land. Now, twenty-fours years later, circumstances were taking him back to Savannah. But he would return as a free man, a man who had learned to read and write even though it was forbidden, a man who was choosing to help Sayre Howard, even though it could cost him plenty. Freeman pondered all this, awed by life's mysterious twists and how long it had taken life to make some small sense to him. He knew he was one of the lucky ones.

"Looks like you're ready," Mr. Overby said. "I don't think we've forgotten anything. Of course, you both have rifles and knives for protection and for foraging. I'm afraid food will be scarce along the way if the Yankees have done what they said they'd do."

"I made a list," Freeman said. "Everything I thought of is here. Miss Sayre, are you ready to go?"

She glanced at the three adults, unsure whether or nor she should confess that she'd added the fiddle, her father's book of Shakespeare with the sketches of Warrior tucked inside, and the box of feathers.

"Give me a few minutes. I need to…" Her voice trailed off as she stooped to collect a bunch of black-eyed Susan she had picked from the roadside.

Sayre carried the bright yellow wildflowers toward the mound of dirt set in the woods that circled the field near the farmhouse. At her mother's grave, she dropped to her knees, placed a flower on the mound, and bent to kiss the sod.

"Good-bye, Mother. We'll come home. Warrior, Freeman, me, and Papa too. I know we'll come back. I only wish you'd be here to hug us."

She rose and walked across Warrior's pasture. She stopped there also, left a flower in the cool grass, and said quietly, "Wait for us."

Her last stop was the house, rather, its remains. She stopped at the brick hearth, which had not burned, and left the last flower there. She touched the blackened bricks and memories of her family peopled the ruins around her: the music and laughter, quiet times listening to her father read. She felt much older than her fourteen years, but certainly not wiser, just a bit more weary and afraid. The driving force behind her departure was the desire to see, touch, and ride Warrior again. She would not be defeated by those thieving Yankees, and she would do everything in her power to bring her horse home.

She turned and walked to the wagon. "I'm ready, Freeman. Not a lot to leave behind."

Mrs. Overby came to Sayre, hugged her, and held her closely. "We'll watch over the farm. That's not a huge chore, I'm afraid. But don't worry, Andrew will check on it often. Remember we love you."

Then Andrew Overby shook Freeman's hand. Though the peculiar significance of the moment was plain to all—a plantation owner's hand extended to, and clasped by, a freed slave—Mr. Overby spoke only of their immediate situation, "You know we don't want Sayre to go, but I respect what you say about freedom only being as good as the important things it lets you do. Still, these are perilous times. You go with our thoughts and our blessings. We'll be here waiting."

Freeman smiled. "Thank you." His voice was low and firm. Then he turned to Sayre, "Ready?"

The girl climbed onto the wagon. Freeman grabbed the reins and clucked to Beauty. The old mule marched into a strong trot and they were off. Sayre turned once to wave a final good-bye as the road arched and the farm disappeared.

Feeling the need to lighten the mood, and wanting to resolve an important issue, Freeman cleared his throat, "You know, Miss Sayre, I can't be calling you 'Miss Sayre.' Here you are working so hard to look like a boy—and doing a pretty good job—and one 'Miss Sayre' out of me could ruin it all. I was thinking I might call you 'Johnny' or 'Billy' or maybe something jaunty like 'Stubby' or…"

Sayre's laughter cut him short. A mischievous grin still lit up his face.

"Just 'Sayre' will do. You're right about leaving off the 'Miss,' but I think 'Sayre' is fine."

"And easy to remember," concluded Freeman with a chuckle.

The road from the farm led to a town called Louisville, the same name as the city in her father's beloved Kentucky. He had been born in Harrodsburg, which lay about thirty miles south of Lexington. It was an old town nestled in the heart of horse country, where Saddlebreds and Thorough-breds bounded in pastures filled with sweet-smelling grass, so deeply colored by the limestone beneath, it was almost blue. He had been taught to ride when he was ten and later apprenticed to the Pleasant Hill Shakers to learn their style of carpentry, revered throughout the region for its artistry. And learn it he did, well enough to establish his own successful business. He'd met Sayre's mother in London, Kentucky, while he was building the first of his magnificent staircases in her father's home. The couple married a year later, and for a reason Sayre had never known, they decided to move to Georgia. There they'd bought their small farm with money given to them by her mother's family- a dowry.

Sayre had been her Mother's maiden name and the name of a college for women in Kentucky, which her grandfather had founded. That was all Sayre knew of that piece of family history.

Quickly her mind flashed from thoughts of Kentucky back to Georgia and the road they were traveling. Sayre knew this road well, but now it bore the unsettling signs of the Union Army's march. The way was strewn with abandoned gear, garbage, and the occasional carcass of a cow or pig or, less frequently, a horse. Whenever Sayre saw one of these, her heart contracted as they came closer, fearing that it would be Warrior. Yet somehow she was certain he was traveling far away from her, with part of an army that was now advancing toward Savannah.

About midday, Freeman pulled the wagon to a halt by a creek and unhitched Beauty to let her graze nearby. He and Sayre sat down to eat the bread and cheese Mrs. Overby had prepared and to feast on her homemade apple cobbler.

"Not a bad beginning," Sayre ventured, her mouth stuffed with cobbler.

"They're fine folks. None better. Your pa said that."

"He sure did, and, as always, he knew people, could spot the good and the bad. If he caught a whiff of bad, he'd refuse the work. I remember a man from Sandersville who wanted a sideboard built, very fancy, very expensive, burled walnut or something like that. My father refused the work. He said he just had a bad feeling about that man. Sure enough, we later learned he'd run off with a lot of money from the bank he owned. Left quite a few farmers in trouble. He was caught and, I think, lynched. Guess they were pretty mad."

"I 'member hearing about him. Your pa did what he felt was right. Stood up for what he believed even if it cost him money. I've learned a lot from him."

Freeman got to his feet, and went to get Beauty. "Now, my four-legged friend, we've all had lunch. We're ready to go again," he said and threw the harness over the mule's wide shoulders as he and Sayre climbed back into the wagon.

CHAPTER 8

Without warning, the full horror of war began to unfold. As they neared Louisville the devastation visited upon Georgia became widespread. Women holding children by their side stood near the road crying, their farmhouses in ruins behind them. Animals lay dead or dying in the fields. Except for the weeping, there were few sounds other than the steady clump, clump of Beauty's hooves. As they rounded a bend in the road, Sayre put her hand on Freeman's arm.

"Let's stop now," she said, "just this once, please."

Freeman pulled Beauty to a halt beside an old woman and two small boys. All three were simply sitting on the stone steps of what had once been their cabin. Beside them lay the body of a huge red bloodhound, a gaping bullet wound in his side. The woman stroked his limp head.

Freeman and Sayre got out of the wagon and walked over to her. Freeman broke the silence. "Can we help, ma'am?"

"Reckon not," she said slowly as the younger boy snuggled close to her and hid his face in the sleeve of her dress. "They killed ol' Tom. Just right out shot 'im. He didn't even bark at 'em. I tried to call 'im back when he went to sniff 'em and then one pulled a gun and shot 'im. They said they was sure he was one of those Georgia bloodhounds that used to chase the runaway slaves. It weren't so. He was just an old huntin' dog my husband loved more than anything."

Her voice was barely more than a whisper. "More than anything. Don't know what we're goin' to do. My man is

47

fightin' with General Lee, same as my son—he's pa to these little fellas, and the only thing we got left is a few sweet taters the Yankees didn't find." Her eyes filled with tears and both small boys began to sob.

Sayre sat beside her. She looked at the dead dog and offered, "We've got a shovel. Could we help bury him?"

The woman looked up and nodded. Sayre went to the wagon to get the shovel as Freeman picked up the animal. "Where should we put him, ma'am?" he asked.

Looking unsure what to do with her hands now that the dog was out of reach, the woman numbly replied, "Over there. That was his favorite spot. Loved to lie in the shade of that old oak and wait for my husband to finish plowin'. Then they'd go off into the woods to get dinner. At night he'd just bay at the stars."

Freeman laid the dog under the tree and began digging the grave. Sayre stood beside him. The old woman and the two boys sat very still, not venturing near the spot. When the hole was deep enough, Freeman and Sayre lifted the dog's body and set it down in the red Georgia clay. She touched the hound's wrinkled forehead, then quickly ran to the wagon, returning with a feather from the box. She laid it beside the dog and lowered her head.. As each shovelful of dirt closed the grave, Sayre thought of her mother and how the same sound had ended a part of her girlhood that had been warm and comforting. For a moment she forgot where she was and had to blink to realize what was happening.

"Sayre," Freeman spoke, then added so softly that only she would hear, "Miss Sayre, it's time to go."

"Of course," she replied and walked to the family. "I'm so sorry," she said, "for all of us."

The grandmother looked up, nodded, and closed her arms more tightly around her two grandsons.

CHAPTER 9

*S*ayre and Freeman were silent as they continued their
journey through the countryside. It was deathly still
for November. Even the birds and squirrels were silent. Sayre
was astonished at how quickly she had become accustomed
to the death and sadness that surrounded them. Neither she
nor Freeman had spoken any more about the bloodhound,
but they knew they couldn't stop again to help anyone. They
had to keep pace with the army, even as they remained a
good distance from the rear. Additionally, they didn't have
enough food to share with the huge numbers of people in
need. The disaster was simply too great. Still, Sayre took
some bleak comfort in the solace they had given to one old
woman and two young boys.

It was evening when they approached Louisville. They
smelled the smoke before they saw the charred town lying
innocently on either side of the road. Freeman guided
Beauty down its main street. Debris littered the road lined
with blackened, looted stores. Sayre pulled her hat down farther over her eyes as a man approached. He was carrying a
rifle.

"You from around here, son?"

Sayre spoke. "Yes, sir. My man here is taking me to my
aunt in Savannah. All the other slaves ran off after Sherman's
men burned our house. My daddy's fighting with Lee. My
mother's dead. Any Yankees around?"

"No, son. They came. Burned everything they could, drank our whiskey, terrorized the women and children, and left about three days ago. You ought to be careful. Lots of our cavalry out there and some too-young soldiers. Better camp close to town tonight. There's one house left standing over there. Might let you stay. Lady of the house is lettin' others camp there."

"Thank you," Sayre said.

Freeman clucked to Beauty and turned the wagon toward a distant brick structure barely visible in the growing darkness and overhanging haze of smoke.

"Maybe they'll let us camp in their barn," Sayre wished out loud. "I confess, I like having a roof over my head."

Suddenly she saw movement in the road ahead. She grabbed Freeman's arm. "Whoa. Stop. There's something lying in the road. Do you see it?"

Freeman halted the wagon and they both strained to see what Sayre had noticed.

"Looks like a dog, a big one," Freeman finally said. "Looks like he's sick or hurt."

Sayre jumped down. "I'll have a closer look. We can go around him, but I think he's alive. I'm sure I saw him move. Don't worry. I'll be careful."

Freeman guided the wagon to the side of the road, then got out. He picked up his gun and walked to where Sayre was studying the wounded animal.

She looked up as he approached and said, "She hasn't been shot. Looks like a wagon wheel hit her in the head. Do you think she'll let us get closer?"

"Don't know, Sayre, but let's be careful. It looks bad. I can finish her off. Don't want the poor creature to suffer no more."

"I know. I keep thinking of the bloodhound back there," Sayre said as she stepped closer to the bleeding animal.

The large yellow dog raised her head, but didn't snarl or growl, just looked at them, the huge gash in her head laid open. Sayre stooped and tentatively touched her heaving body. No response. She looked at Freeman.

"All right," he said. "If she'll let me, I'll put her in the back of the wagon. Let me see if I can pick her up without her bitin' me. You know wounded animals can be dangerous."

Freeman slipped his arms under the dog, making sure her head didn't drop, then lifted her effortlessly and gingerly carried her to the wagon where Sayre was unfolding a roughly woven woolen blanket that the Overbys had given them. The dog lay quietly, but her breathing came in quick spurts.

"We'll see what more we can do when we stop for the night," Freeman said climbing back into the wagon.

Sayre slipped in beside him. She was quiet, determined to keep an eye on the animal to see if the movement of the wagon caused her more pain. Sayre's thoughts were of Warrior. Was he somewhere hurt? Would a stranger stop and care for him?

When they reached the gate to the large brick house, they saw that the yard was filled with small bands of people preparing campfires for the evening. It was unclear to Sayre if they were locals or travelers. Either way, they wore the now-familiar look of those who had lost everything. Some would be headed to the homes of friends or relatives to piece their lives back together. Others were probably hoping to survive right here somehow.

Sayre jumped down and walked up to an elderly man who was standing with a young woman and five small children. All looked thin. Their clothes and faces were dirty.

"Excuse me, but is someone in charge here?"

"Yep," the man replied, "that woman over there. She owns this place. Nice lady. Says we can stay a spell. Mighty nice of her to allow folks like us around. Says the only reason her house was left standing was that some of Sherman's staff stayed here. They'd be the villains who stood and watched their troops loot and burn the town," he finished bitterly.

Sayre thanked him, then walked toward a tall woman in a flowing brown dress trimmed with a crisp white lace collar. A rich chocolate-colored shawl was draped over her shoulders and she was deep in conversation with a man dressed in a blue flannel shirt, a faded coat and trousers. Sayre waited for them to pause and look her way.

"Hello, and excuse me, ma'am. My name is Sayre Howard." She pointed to Freeman and the wagon, "We would like to camp here if that would be all right."

Then, as if presenting credentials, Sayre repeated the story that explained their circumstances. Finally, thinking it would be an appropriately masculine gesture, she extended her hand and the woman took it.

"Certainly, son. There is a small spot in the shed for you and your slave. We have a well for drinking. My daughters are here helping. Do you have enough blankets? There are so many people in need who have nothing."

"We have enough provisions. Thank you. We just need a safe place to rest."

"We all need that, I'm afraid," she said, and added as her voice dropped, "particularly our boys out there dealing with the Yankees. My name is Mrs. Bryant. Let me know if you need anything."

"Yes, ma'am. We'll just go find that shed. Thank you. This is our first day out. We've come from my farm, over near Griswoldville. Not much left anywhere. It looks like a swarm of locusts went through and ate or killed everything in its path. Same thing must have happened here. Anyway, we appreciate your hospitality."

Sayre turned and motioned for Freeman to follow her. Beauty moved forward slowly and they stopped under some trees near an old shed. Sayre walked into the small structure. It was in good condition with well worn boards that enclosed two stalls and a small room to one side that held a couple of rakes, several hoes and three buckets. She and Freeman unloaded a few items from the wagon, careful not to disturb the dog, who was lying very still.

It didn't take long to settle into the small space that would be theirs for the evening. Without speaking, Freeman opened his knapsack and took out the brown wormwood while Sayre pulled a bucket of water from the well. Together, they began cleaning the dog's wound, all the time wary that their patient might snap at them in pain. But the animal lay still, her eyes closed, her breathing shallow. When the gash was clean, Freeman covered it with his ointment and applied some sulfur to keep the flies away.

Sayre took a mockingbird's feather from her box and laid it beside the sleeping animal. She rested her hand on the dog's body. The dog stirred and then looked at her with wide, dark eyes. Sayre filled a bowl with clean water and held it to the animal's lips. No response. The girl gently opened the dog's mouth and poured in small amounts of water. She swallowed each one. A good sign, Sayre thought.

Freeman helped her gently tuck the blanket around the dog. Then they unhooked Beauty, brushed her, picked her hooves to make sure no stones had lodged there, and led her to the one stall inside Mrs. Bryant's shed. The spunky mule was delighted to find a bale of hay awaiting her and she immediately began munching contentedly. Freeman and Sayre found their own spots, Freeman's nearer the door, his rifle close by. Sayre nestled in blankets Mrs. Overby had given her and the smell made her dream of home, the farm, and Warrior. She was lulled asleep by the murmurs of the people around the campfires outside.

Sometime in the night they were startled awake by a wail that penetrated the night air. It was a deep and sorrowful sound. Sayre bolted up, froze for a moment, struggling to realize where she was, then threw off the covers and stumbled toward the wagon. Freeman was already there, stroking the body of the dog.

"She's all right. Let's hope she's alive tomorrow morning and that wasn't a good-bye."

Sayre added her touch to Freeman's. "I've never heard a dog make that sound." She looked down at the dog, who was now sleeping. "I'd like to take her with us. Maybe she'll bring us luck. We sure could use some." A smile flickered across Sayre's face. "If she makes it, let's call her Lady."

Freeman looked at his companion, a smile dotting the corner of his mouth. He remembered telling Sayre many years ago about the first dog he had loved, a hound who was his treasured companion, following him everywhere on the farm. Like Freeman himself, the dog had belonged to his master, Dr. Thomas. She'd been a magnificent animal, and her name had been Lady.

Chapter 10

As a tenuous morning light trickled into the shed, Sayre stirred, sat up and looked around. Freeman was not in his place by the door. She sniffed the air, smelling the acrid smoke from the ruins that marked a once-thriving Southern town. As she stood up, she remembered the injured dog, and walked quickly toward the wagon. Freeman was hunched over a small fire, a pot of coffee next to him.

"She's still with us," he offered as Sayre appeared. "She must be plenty tough, or my wormwood is mighty good stuff. Been thinking," and he paused to take a sip of the hot coffee, "Lady would be a right good name for her."

Sayre peered inside the wagon and was greeted by two eyes looking back, two eyes that were a little brighter than they'd been yesterday. The dog's soft, thick yellow fur was matted in places with mud from the road. Her huge, black paws were resting on the bed of the wagon.

She gently touched the dog's body. "Guess you made it a bit longer, Lady. It might be rough today, but we'll make you as comfortable as we can. We're on our way to find War-rior, and when you meet him, you'll know why. It's pretty dangerous, but you know that." She turned to Freeman, "Think she'll eat anything?"

"I'm fixing a bit for her. Come and eat yours. Cold bis-cuits again, but the coffee's some of my best. We need to ration the bacon. We'll let Lady build an appetite, then we'll see if she'll eat something."

Suddenly there was the sound of hoofbeats pounding on a nearby street. Freeman and Sayre watched as the throng of people in the yard rose as one and began whooping and hollering, coming to life at the sight of a small band of Confederate cavalry racing by, their horses' hooves kicking up dust.

There were shouts of: "Go get 'em! Get them Yankees! Attaway, boys!"

One man stood waving his hat in the air, tears streaming from his eyes. Within minutes the riders were gone and the camp settled back, though a buzz of excitement remained.

Sayre was quiet. Her eyes had been fixed only on the passing horses. She blinked, then sat down. She and Freeman ate in silence, the enormity of the task they had chosen washing over them.

Sayre finished her breakfast, and when she'd drained the last bit of rich black coffee, she took two small pieces of bacon from the wagon and fried them over the fire. As she carried the meat to Lady, she knew Freeman was watching, but it was her mother's voice she heard, laughingly teasing, "I declare, child, you care more about those animals than you do about yourself!" Sayre fed her patient each slice and the dog took the small pieces of food and then licked Sayre's fingers. She added water to a bowl and Lady drank sparingly. She patted the dog's firm body to let her know she was safe, then went back to the front of the wagon, harnessed Beauty into place, and helped Freeman load up.

Just as they began moving through the yard, a little boy in a faded red shirt came running up. "You takin' Sam's dog, ain't ya!"

Freeman pulled Beauty to a stop and said, "Is Sam around? Guess we won't if she's his dog."

"It's Sam's dog, all right, but he ain't here right now. Gone fightin' with Lee. That there's a good dog. Been sittin' in the road since Sam left about three months ago. She's a good hunter. Mrs. Bryant here is supposed to look after her, but that dog mainly looks after herself."

"Then we'll see what Mrs. Bryant wants us to do," Freeman replied. "Show me where she is. Sure wouldn't want to take anyone's dog."

He got down and followed the boy to where Mrs. Bryant, today wearing a navy dress, was walking through the campsites. The man in the work clothes was again by her side.

"Mrs. Bryant, good morning, ma'am," Freeman called. "This boy tells me that Sayre and I have Sam's dog. Should we leave her here? Dog's been hit hard by something, maybe a wagon. I think we could nurse her back to health on our way to Savannah."

"Yes, that is Sam's dog, but I'd be obliged if you'd take her. It's not that she's a burden, but times are so very hard. She's a good keeper, fends for herself, hunts well. Sam loved her a lot, and I had to shut her up in the shed for a week to keep her from trying to track him after he left. He didn't want to take her into the war. When all this is over, maybe he'll find you in Griswoldville to retrieve that dog, but for now…" Rather than putting the situation into words, the woman concluded with a gesture that took in all the desolation that surrounded them.

"I think the dog'll mend pretty well. If she can hunt, she'll be a help to us, and you can tell Sam to look us up in Griswoldville if we all survive this war. Appreciate the use of the shed. We'll be on our way now."

"You're welcome. Stay safe. It's a different world out there now."

"Yes'm."

Freeman walked back to the wagon and, once in the seat beside Sayre, clucked to Beauty and headed out of Louisville.

Both were silent, lost in their thoughts. For the first time in his life, Freeman felt the hollow feeling of doubt in his ability to solve a problem. He had survived enslavement, had some mighty good luck, had become free again. But this war was creating so many new challenges and so many new victims. Freeman felt deeply the responsibility he'd assumed for the girl who sat at his side, and now there was no turning back, not with Sayre bent on finding Warrior. But he knew that soon the land would become swampy and the streams that crisscrossed their way would become deeper. Most ominously, the Union Army lay ahead, an unknown in a sea of unknowns.

CHAPTER 11

"You know, Freeman," Sayre finally ventured as they plodded slowly along, "I think I'll begin reading *King Lear* to Lady tonight if we find a good place to camp. It's a good story about a king who sees his whole world come apart when his daughters begin to fight over their inheritance. It was one of Papa's favorites. Maybe he saw the war coming and felt a little like the old monarch who was powerless to stop his life from changing.. Anyway, animals like to hear a soft voice. Maybe it'll help Lady heal."

"Could be," Freeman responded absentmindedly, his eyes intent on the road and the wrecked land it traversed. "I'm just wonderin' when we're gonna catch up with some Yankees or even some Confederates. Or when one of them is gonna catch up with us. All I see are houses burned to the ground or robbed of all that folks had, rich and poor. And more dead horses, cattle, and hogs than I can count. The only things that left are the chimneys, tall and black."

"Like forgotten sentinels," Sayre chimed in. "Like monuments to a time when our world is turned upside down and humans only settle their differences by destroying. Sometimes when Papa's friends talked about the war, it seemed glorious, fighting for a cause and they_"

"Whoa, hold on, Sayre," Freeman said. "We gotta stop a minute. Beauty's limping. Could be a stone in her hoof. Let's pull over and I'll pick around to see what's there."

When the wagon stopped, Sayre leapt to the ground and said, "You stay here. I'll check."

She lifted Beauty's leg to have a look. Sure enough the culprit was a rock wedged neatly between her hoof and the shoe. Sayre took a knife from her pocket and eased the pebble out, checked to see if there was a cut, returned the leg to the ground, and rubbed it gently.

"You are a fine animal, Beauty," she whispered to the mule as she rubbed her neck. "We're gonna find Warrior. I know you'll help. He's nearby. I believe that so much I_"

"Shh."Freeman came up beside her. "There's a group comin' down the road. Haven't seen us yet. Looks like they're Confederates, but you can never tell. You stay here. I'll head down to talk to 'em"

Freeman walked down the road and stopped as the six men approached. They were ragged and looked half-starved. Three of the men each carried a small girl on his back. When they drew near Freeman, the men shifted the children to the ground where the little ones stood looking up at the tall black man. They held tightly onto the hands of the soldiers.

Freeman said, "I picked some apples from a tree we found along the road. They're in the wagon over yonder. Looks like you and the young ones here could use them."

"Mighty nice of you," the leader said.

The other soldiers shuffled and stood silently by.

"We've been feedin' on raw turnips, meat skins and parched corn. And that's on a good day. Sometimes it's just roots from the woods. These little gals are hungry. We found 'em in a mud-chinked log cabin back there."

Freeman knelt to be eye level with the children, "How old are you?"

There was no reply.

"Not sure," responded the soldier. "I'm guessing the little ones are three or four, the older one five or six maybe.

They was wearing these dirty cotton dresses. Just sacks with holes ripped out for their arms, really. No other living creature around. These two was hiding in a smoke cellar. The other'n was in a bush near what had been a well. They ain't said a word since. We tried to leave 'em with some neighbors, but those ladies said they didn't know how they was gonna feed their own children, and couldn't add three more to their brood, so we just brought 'em with us. We fed 'em and washed them, clothes and all, in a creek near their cabin, but, as you can see, it didn't help much."

"We just came from Louisville," Freeman said. "It's not too far from here. There's a Mrs. Bryant in the town. She owns one of the only houses still standing after Sherman came through. I bet she could help you."

"That devil Sherman. He's the reason we's headin' home. No use fightin' anymore. We need to find out what's happened to our families, our farms. What you two doin' out here?"

One little girl pulled on the soldier's arm, and he reached down and lifted her up. She rested her head on his shoulder.

He shifted his weight. "So where are you two headed?"

"Savannah. The other slaves left, but I said I'd get this boy delivered safe to his relatives."

"I got a couple of hands I hope is still on my farm in Sandersville." There was a slight, awkward pause. "I'll be glad to take some of those apples thank you. We'll move along. We got a long way to go."

"Just come on to the wagon and we can get those apples."

When they came close to the spot where Sayre and Lady were waiting, Freeman said, "Sayre, this man is gonna take a few of our apples."

Sayre moved to the rear of the wagon, took out a burlap sack and handed it to the soldier. This gave her a closer look at the child he held. Sayre wanted to reassure the little girl that she was in safe hands, but was hesitant to touch her, not wanting to scare her. Her dark hair was knotted and she was covered in dust. Sayre hoped Mrs. Bryant would have the chance to give these little ones some care, some food, and a thorough washing.

"Well, I thank you," the soldier said, re-shifting the child in his arms. "The Union Army's not too far up ahead. We skirted 'round, but be careful. Kilpatrick's cavalry is operating all round these parts. Wheeler's cavalry's giving him a run for his money. Still, our boys ain't no match for the new repeating rifles the Yankees have. This here fightin' is gonna end soon. Ain't seen nothing like their army."

"Thanks for the warning," Freeman said. "At least you've rescued these three little ones. We're glad to see something good along this road. Don't forget about Mrs. Bryant. I hope she can help."

Sayre and Freeman watched as the soldiers lifted the girls to their backs and trudged toward Louisville. Then Freeman got back in the wagon, clucked to Beauty and they moved cautiously down the now-deserted red clay road.

For that night's campsite, they chose a creek in thick woods a good distance from the road. Freeman carefully hid the wagon in the middle of a huge stand of tall river cane. After the soldier's warning that both Union and Confederate cavalry were operating in the area, there was no question of lighting a fire, so Sayre quietly re-dressed Lady's wound with cool water from the swiftly flowing stream and let her rest. Dinner was small chunks of bread and cheese washed down by creek water. The last of the apples added a few more nutrients to their meager meal. Going hungry was routine now, and the travelers felt lucky to have what little food they had.

The air was chilly and the sky was brilliant with sparkling stars. Beauty was tethered to a tree and had found something to munch on after her ration of corn. Sayre sat in the back of the wagon with Lady. Freeman relaxed on the ground, his back against a wagon wheel.

"I guess I won't read tonight. No fire. No light. Let's see, I could tell Lady about King Lear or let her know about Warrior and what we're doing," Sayre mused.

"That's a good idea. I bet she's wondering what she's gotten herself into and who these two crazy people are. Maybe she's even thinkin' of headin' back to Louisville where sane people live."

As Sayre stroked her face, Lady stirred and placed one huge paw on the girl's leg.

"Well, Lady, just to let you in on a secret, all we want to do is find the most beautiful horse in the world. Wait until you see him! He's the color of sunshine and he has the biggest, darkest eyes you've ever seen. Later, when you're up and about and Warrior is back safe with us, we'll ride through the woods and you can chase squirrels and rabbits, even foxes, if you want. And Freeman and Papa will rebuild the farmhouse. It'll be like it was before. Almost."

Sayre stopped. Without her mother, that thought held no promise. Freeman said nothing.

Hoofbeats approaching from behind startled them. Freeman rose, his rifle cocked.

"Shh, shh," he whispered as he hurried to grab Beauty's lead line and lead her behind the wall of river cane.

Sayre shuddered when she heard gunfire as the riders drew near. She ducked her head onto Lady's body and lay very still for a moment. But her curiosity overcame her fear and she carefully peered over the side of the wagon.

The mounted soldiers thundered through the woods at breakneck speed. There were about ten men in blue uniforms leaning close to their horses' necks to avoid the low-hanging branches. They didn't see the two travelers, the wagon, or the mule. The creek water shuddered with the impact of the pounding hooves as they galloped away across the field and into the next patch of trees.

The last horse, carrying his blue-clad rider, was magnificent, muscled beyond anything Sayre had ever seen. His strides were long, sure. He was a seasoned warhorse carrying his rider effortlessly. He plunged into the woods as bullets from unseen pursuers sprayed around him. He was confident and took the creek in one bound, soaring across it and landing ready to conquer the field ahead.

Sayre stared, transfixed. She knew this horse and loved his power, now fully unleashed. Warrior had materialized before her eyes. Before she knew what she was doing, she stood up and jumped from the wagon and began walking toward the creek. Warrior was alive, but no longer hers.

Behind her now came more cavalry, this time in lighter-colored uniforms. These men fired repeatedly at the fleeing soldiers swerving through the trees. They were traveling so fast and so intently, they didn't notice her concealed by the trees.

Then the hoofbeats died away and Sayre and Freeman remained statue-like, not daring to believe what had just happened. Tears flooded from Sayre's eyes. Freeman looked at the ground. Beauty nudged his arm.

Minutes passed. Sayre walked to the edge of the creek and dipped her hand into the cold water letting it linger on her skin. Then she returned to the wagon and pulled a quilt from the chest. She stood for a moment, clutching the quilt, before climbing back into the wagon. She lay down on the rough boards, pulled the quilt over her, and snuggled next to Lady. The smell of the animal's fur was comforting. Sayre closed her eyes and saw only Warrior. When she finally fell asleep, she was traveling fast and far astride her horse. Warrior's soft face and strong body were alive in her dreams.

CHAPTER 12

The smell of coffee awakened her from a sound sleep. Lady lay next to her breathing softly. The dog stirred, then settled back to sleep as Sayre climbed down from the wagon to join Freeman at the morning cook-fire.

He handed her a plate and a mug and she ate hungrily as he sipped his coffee. Lady sat up, whined, then lay back down, and Freeman moved to the wagon and handed her a piece of beef jerky and a chunk of bread. He took the wormwood from his knapsack and rubbed it deeply in her wound. Lady only stared up at him, the jerky still in her mouth. She was a good patient, uncomplaining. He walked to the creek, dipped some water into a blue crockery bowl and came back to the dog.

"Look at you, old girl," he cooed. "You're gonna get better, and when Mr. Howard sees you, he will wanna know your pedigree. Yessir. You're a mighty fine animal. So when are you gonna get outta that wagon and earn your keep by chasing down some squirrels or a fat raccoon? We're countin' on you, you know."

He laid his hand on her body and stroked her. "Been a long time since we had a dog," he said.

Freeman moved to sit next to Sayre. His brow was furrowed. "Sayre, it's mighty dangerous out here. This is not a story in one of your books. We could both get killed. There ain't no rules now, especially for civilians like us. General

Sherman's seen to that. It's survival. So I'm sayin' we should turn around and head home, work for Mr. Overby until your papa comes walking down the road..."

"And give up Warrior as lost?"

"Maybe so. At least you know he's made it this far all right. The world has plans of its own so no amount of interfering on our part will change that. Maybe it wasn't meant to be. Maybe your three years with Warrior was all you was to have, like my six with my son, Jeb. I lost him and my wife. Maybe now you've lost Warrior."

Sayre was silent. How could she go "home"? It was just a place now, a dot on a map. Who was there? If she went back to the farm, she would wonder about Warrior every day. While on this quest, there was a chance of finding him; to end the search would mean she had given up Warrior forever. What would life be without him? She bowed her head. Freeman was right, she knew. He was a kind and wise man who had her best interests at heart. He was always pragmatic, that was the word, one of her father's favorites. It meant that Freeman did what was practical without a lot of emotion. But Sayre knew in her soul that she would not and could not abandon Warrior.

She looked up. "You go home if you want. I have to follow him. I know how dangerous this is. I learned that lesson last night. War is certainly no fairy tale. It may have even taken Papa away forever. Maybe that's why I have to at least try to bring Warrior home alive. You take Lady home."

Sayre rose and went to the wagon, put her book of Shakespeare and her precious box of feathers into her knapsack, threw it over her shoulder, and picked up a quilt, which she clutched to her breast.

"I don't know where I'm going, but I know I can't go home. You've been a good friend to us all, and you're certainly not beholden to me or to anyone. I know that. Why should you get killed? A black man now is safer than most anyone."

She turned and walked doggedly toward the road. Adrenalin raced through her body and doubt filled her every pore. She held the quilt as if it had something in it, an injured animal, a lost dream maybe, and she began to talk to Warrior, and to the god or gods who ruled the universe, trying to gather courage and direction. She felt small and insignificant until she saw the red feather in the road, a gift from a cardinal that had flown this way. She stopped, knelt, picked it up, and felt its soft edges in her hand.

She said in a hushed voice, "I know, Papa. You're here. We are on the right path. Please stay with me and guide me to Warrior. I will do whatever it takes. I love you."

She was so lost in thought , she didn't hear the wagon pull up beside her. She turned to see Lady sitting for the first time in the seat next to the strong black man. Sayre looked into Freeman's eyes and saw the determination there. Wordlessly, she climbed into the wagon and kissed Lady's neck.

CHAPTER 13

The rain began the next afternoon-cold, strong and steady. Sayre and Freeman donned their rain gear and covered the supplies and Lady with an oilcloth. Lady was once again lying in the back of the wagon as sitting up seemed to tire her. Beauty slogged through the mud. Several times, Freeman stopped as the wagon became mired in a rut that held one of the wheels captive. Whenever this happened, Sayre and Freeman both pushed from behind as Freeman clucked to Beauty to move forward. By rocking back and forth and then placing a board they carried in the back for just such emergencies, the little wagon would lurch out as Beauty waited for them to once again clamber into their seats.

When a deserted barn came into view, Freeman did not hesitate to escape the weather. Sayre led Lady into one stall and Beauty into another. Freeman secured the building, checking every corner, and finding the remains of one hay bale in the loft. The adjacent cabin had been burned, but the barn was intact. No livestock were anywhere to be seen. There was no sign of life.

Freeman braved the rain to gather stones, which could surround a fire in the lean-to attached to the barn. As Sayre felt its warmth, she was glad they'd gathered wood before the storm hit. Still energized by seeing Warrior, she was restless and, while Freeman cooked a squirrel he had shot, she ventured out and found a creek. Despite the rain, she lay in the cold water, letting it cascade over her, and looked up at the darkening sky. At the edge of the bank was a patch of cardinal flowers, their vibrant red color awash in the fading light. 'With the first frost they'll be gone,' she thought and continued lying in the water until her body, responding to the cold, said it was time to return to reality. She stood, gathered her clothes, rinsed them in the creek and put on the extra pair of her father's baggy overalls and the two spare shirts she'd brought with her. As she dashed back to the barn, it occurred to her that she probably did not run like a boy. So, to Freeman's amusement, she practiced walking to and fro in the barn, trying to settle on what a boy's gait should be. It was good to laugh, but they both knew they were surely getting close to the Union Army, which meant that her disguise was essential to her safety, to their safety.

Lady was growing stronger and could now stand and walk. Tonight, she sat next to Sayre as she read *King Lear* aloud, taking on different voices for the many characters. Sayre found that reading helped her forget how hungry she was. The foraging by ravenous soldiers and desperate civilians had consumed more than just cultivated crops and livestock: it had also decimated the natural world so that Freeman's traps often stayed empty, hunting was unreliable, and even wild onions and greens were scarce. With autumn ending, the search for edible plants would not get easier.

As they waited in the barn for the skies to clear, Freeman thought of his own little cabin. Perhaps some unknown travelers were sheltering there this very night; maybe they'd build a fire in the fireplace, maybe sit in his rocking chair. He then thought how glad he was that this abandoned barn had been built well, with no leaks or cracks. He listened while Sayre read until the fire died down. As the darkness enfolded them all, Sayre and Lady nestled snugly together in the corner of the barn, and Freeman rested where he could keep an eye on Beauty and their wagon.

On the fourth day, the sun came out and a swift breeze greeted them. It was time to move on. They were getting ready to enter swamp country, where the land changed, the forest thinned, and the tidal streams were unusually treacherous because it was difficult to estimate the depth of their dark waters. One thing was certain, the fall rains had added to those depths.

Lady now sat straight and tall between Sayre and Freeman, her black muzzle pointing down the road, her dark eyes alert. She had even barked one night at some strange sound she heard. A good sign, Sayre thought, for it was the only sound the dog had made except for her wail on the night they rescued her.

The first indication that they were catching up to the Union army was the array of black men, women, and children, moving slowly down the road ahead. Sayre pulled her hat low over her cropped hair as Freeman guided Beauty into the back of the crowd. He slowed next to a woman carrying a large bundle on her back, with five little children beside and behind her. They ranged in age from about three to thirteen, the oldest somewhere near Sayre's age.

"Would you like to put the little ones onboard? You can put your bundle there too if you'd like," Freeman offered.

The woman turned, glared at Sayre, and shook her head. "We've run away from his kind. Don't need no help. Following the Yanks to Mr. Lincoln's house. We're free now." She added reproachfully, "You should do the same."

"I am free," Freeman responded. "Just taking this boy to his aunt. His mother's dead and his father freed me before going to fight. Reckon I owe him this trip. Your husband around?"

"Sure is. Up front making sure the army can get down the road. He's working with a whole bunch of the Yanks. We're on our way to Savannah. My name's Sally and I reckon I'm much obliged to put my littlest ones on the wagon now that I know your story."

Beauty halted as four of the children jumped onto the back of the wagon, their faces lit up by the prospect of a ride.

Sayre turned around. "I'm Sayre. Pleased to meet you. Glad we could give you a ride. This is Lady. We found her. She was hit by a wagon, hurt badly. That's why she has this big cut on her head."

"We had a huge brown dog on the plantation," one small girl murmured, "but we had to leave him behind when we ran away. I guess the Yanks got him. I like Lady. She's got a nice face. My pa says we're heading north, wherever that is. You going there too?"

"Sort of, but only as far as Savannah. My aunt's there. Where was your plantation?"

Her mother answered quickly, "None of your business. We all ran away. That's enough."

Chastened, Sayre responded, "You're right. Sorry, I have no business knowing."

As they rode down the road, blacks from nearby farms joined the steady stream of refugees, all driven by a desire to escape their enslavement and begin a new life within the confines of the Union Army. Most were walking with very few provisions.

"I wonder how far ahead the Union Army is, Freeman," Sayre said, then stopped suddenly and turned. She'd heard the sound of horses behind them, horses moving at a fast pace.

The throng of people choking the road quickly moved to one side to allow these Union soldiers to pass. Their leader, an older man with a definite air of authority, began yelling at the people lining either side of the road.

"Clear the way and that's an order," he shouted. "Confederates are behind us. Let us through. Let us through, I said." He turned to his men. "Hurry up. We've got to catch up with the other division. We'll never get to Savannah at this pace. Faster. Move these blacks out of the way." To the crowd watching in dread, he shouted, " Let my men through. Go home!"

His huge horse, sweating even in the chilly air, plunged through the lines of terrified blacks, clearing a path for his soldiers. Women clutched their children as the riders moved with speed and purpose, never really seeing the fear, hope and desperation on the faces surrounding them. Still, as the soldiers passed through the crowd, a cheer slowly rose. It began quietly, almost a somber salute, but soon it gained momentum and filled the air. It was a cheer for the end of an inhumane way of life that was slowly dying at the hands of these young, tired soldiers wearing faded blue uniforms and holding a nation's destiny in their hands.

Sayre held Lady close to her. Sally had climbed onto the wagon and was waving her bonnet and joining in the celebration, her children standing, cheering. Freeman sat quietly talking to Beauty, his hat resting on his knee.

By the time all the troops had passed, the crowd had once again grown quiet. They slowly began to follow the army once again. Only this time their pace was quickly outdistanced by the accelerated progress of the soldiers.

As dusk fell, the weary travelers set up their camps within the woods. They cooked their meager dinners and settled down to sleep. Freeman tethered Beauty to the wagon to graze and sat beneath a nearby tree. Sayre and Lady lay in the back of the wagon, huddling together for warmth.

"Sayre," Freeman said quietly. "I'll be right here. Lots of strangers around tonight. Best I stay awake for a while. Most of these folks are good, but there could be a bad one or two hereabouts."

"Thank you, Freeman," she whispered as she pulled the quilt over her. "If you want, Lady and I can keep watch, too. I'm not sleepy tonight."

"It'll be fine. I'll wake you if I need you."

Gradually, the fires died out and the woods were filled only with the night sounds of animals.

Freeman sat very still, his rifle at his side, and only spoke once to a set of footsteps coming closer to the wagon. "That's far enough. The boy's asleep, but I'm not." His voice carried authority; the click of his rifle carried a warning.

CHAPTER 14

$\mathcal{T}$he next day broke overcast, with rain clouds piling on the horizon. Breakfast for Sayre and Freeman was hurried and very sparse—they existed now on black coffee, bits of beef jerky, and whatever edible plants they could find. After carefully repacking, they began another day on the road.

Lady could walk beside the wagon now, but after four miles Freeman lifted her into the seat, afraid she would get lost in the throngs of people who trudged along determined to keep up with the Union soldiers, whom they considered saviors. The Emancipation Proclamation had freed all slaves, but many had not known about the decree until the Union Army began its march through the South. The invasion became the blacks' opportunity to flee their masters. Unfortunately, most slaves had no education and no idea what freedom meant, no concept of how they might begin an independent life. They followed the troops, hoping the soldiers might provide some guidance, some protection from an alien world. But General Sherman's army had neither the time nor the inclination to take on the burden of such desperate and unmoored people. The Union Army's duty was to President Lincoln and its job was to defeat the Confederacy.

Rumors raced through the crowd that Confederate troops were operating in the area, troops that would send former slaves back to their masters, or simply kill them. There were constant murmurs of fear as people jostled to stay near the middle of the crowd, the safest spot to be in case of attack. Freeman, instead, held Beauty at the back of the line and maintained a steady pace, his eyes ever vigilant for signs of trouble.

By the middle of the day, they had crossed several creeks that were overflowing their banks. Clearly, recent rains had been unusually heavy. The gentle landscape allowed these streams to spread wide, remaining shallow enough to be forded.

It was early afternoon when the column slowed, then stopped. Freeman pulled the wagon to a halt, jumped down, and walked to the front of the line. There he saw a swollen stream that cut a narrow channel between two hillsides. These high banks had contained the flooding, resulting in a deep, turbulent current. In peacetime, the road had crossed this gully on a wooden bridge, but that span now lay in ruins, evidently destroyed by the fleeing Rebels. Slightly to its left, Union soldiers stood guard at a new pontoon bridge they had erected during the night.

The Union officer in charge yelled, "Move aside! There's a corps behind you that has to get across. Men, equipment, and livestock will be here shortly. Camp beside the road or in the woods. We'll be here awhile."

Freeman returned to his companions and adeptly maneuvered the wagon through the trees to a clearing that held a bit of grass for Beauty. Sayre and Lady climbed down. Freeman unhooked Beauty and tethered her to the wagon with enough line for her to graze. Although they had brought some hay with them, and occasionally found bales along the way, they knew to use it sparingly. Their corn, too, was running low. This was a perfect chance for Beauty to catch up on some much-needed grazing.

The troops that began arriving were strong, young, lean, and looked well fed from months of foraging in the Confederates' breadbasket. They kept their eyes straight ahead, not looking at the black throng that whispered as they marched by. Next came wagonloads of supplies, then wagons filled with the wounded, and finally a herd of healthy-looking cows and pigs so numerous Sayre could not begin to count them. Most, she thought, had been stolen from the land they had conquered. Her thoughts flew to her papa and the Confederate forces. Were they this well supplied or had Sherman successfully cut off their food and equipment? If so, how long could the Confederate states last under such a siege?

Even though she and Freeman had been on the road only a short time, Sayre was reluctantly concluding that even if it meant defeat, this war must not go on much longer, not with all the suffering she had seen. She had heard that President Lincoln was a fair man and she hoped he would not seek revenge on her homeland, that he would, instead, understand what had led the South to launch this conflict. When the war ended, maybe her father and Warrior would come home. But this was almost too much to wish for just now, so she tucked her fierce hope deep inside.

The crowd settled down to a day of waiting near the raging water for their chance to cross. Folks familiar with the area said this was Ebenezer Creek, usually a docile, insignificant stream. It was hard to imagine it docile or insignificant now that the autumn rains had whipped it into a frenzy.

Sally was talking with people she'd met along the way, her little ones playing on the grass nearby. As the last Union ranks approached, Freeman hitched Beauty to the wagon and he, Sayre, and Lady moved back onto the edge of the road to wait. By dusk the army and their supplies were on the other side, so the crowd began to move to the water's edge.

Suddenly, an officer appeared on the far bank of the stream and commanded his men, "Cut loose the pontoon!"

A wail from the blacks filled the air, fell in disbelief, then rose again. Freeman boldly moved Beauty forward.

He yelled across the raging water, "Sir, please let us pass. I am Freeman, a freed slave with my old master's son. We're goin' to Savannah. We must get across."

As he was talking he was moving Beauty, the wagon, Sayre, and Lady onto the bridge, a move that was confident and stealthy at the same time. Would the officer cut the bridge and kill a black man and young white boy here in front of the troops and the throng of onlookers? Sayre bent her head down, her arm tightening around Lady. The wagon moved forward slowly across the creaking pontoons. A line of people followed, seizing their only chance to rejoin the Union Army. The stream was wide, made even wider now by the rains. It seemed ages before Beauty's hooves touched the firm soil on the other side of the creek. Sayre let out her breath. She saw Freeman's tight face relax slightly.

"That's all that can cross," the officer bellowed. "Stay where you are. We are now cutting the pontoon."

He gave a nod to the soldier on the bank, who quickly cut the lines, causing the bridge to collapse. The blacks on the bridge were thrown into the water. They flailed in the current, struggling against its force. Several Union soldiers rushed to the stream bank and began hauling the frightened people ashore. A woman and a man hurtled downstream and disappeared beneath the dark waters. The dim light prevented anyone from seeing if they surfaced. On the other side of the creek, many of the blacks fell to their knees, praying for those lost in the torrent and also to remain safe from their masters or Confederate soldiers who would surely take them back into bondage, their freedom so short-lived.

Sayre and Freeman had jumped from the wagon and were frantically grabbing hands, shoulders, legs, to haul the drenched people from the water. Among them Sayre spotted Sally, valiantly thrusting her terrified children toward the shore, the baby clinging to her neck and howling at the top of his lungs. Sayre raced to the water's edge, stretching out her hand. Lady ran beside her and as Sayre wrenched each of Sally's children from the water, Lady grabbed a piece of their clothing and helped pull them toward safety. With this exertion, the dog's wound opened a bit and blood again started seeping out onto the fur of her face.

Just as Sayre extended her hand to pluck the baby from Sally's arm, a piece of the bridge struck the woman, knocking her little one from her arms. Sally shrieked and dove for the child, but the tiny body was carried away from her, his dark head bobbing in the white foam. On pure instinct, Sayre dove into the water, swam a few strokes and reached the child. Her only thought was to get the baby to shore. Holding his head above the water, she kicked toward the bank. Freeman was there and he stretched to grab the baby, then pass him to the desperate mother, who had fallen to her knees as her other four children gathered around her.

With the baby safe, Freeman yelled, "Sayre! Here! Take my hand! Take my hand!"

Sayre reached up for him, but the loose pontoon spun around and again struck her, pushing her under the water. She sank, and the rushing water closed over her head.

Underneath, all she heard was the muted rushing of water above her. Sayre began to think, Don't panic. Remember what Papa said: "Keep your feet up and pointed downstream so they don't get trapped in rocks below." She felt cold and somehow calm. Drowning, she mused beneath the raging water, is a solitary death. Will I die here? Now? Alone?

Miraculously, she surfaced and began bobbing up and down, sometimes submerged, sometimes gasping for breath above the churning stream. Ahead of her, a branch hung low over the creek. Sayre maneuvered her body and grabbed at it, missing it the first time but then hooking her arm over it as the water carried her beneath it. She clung to it, coughing and spewing water but glad to at least have her head above the current. She felt terribly cold and dimly alarmed that her fingers and toes were already numb. She had to get to dry land. Suddenly, there was a cracking sound. The branch was breaking slowly. As it broke, Sayre reasoned that at least she could use it to stay afloat. When it snapped, the force hurled her back and under the waves, filling her nose with water. The current threw her again above the surface and she caught one breath before it pushed her back under.

Her thoughts now were on Warrior. She might never see him again, but that would almost be all right. She had tried to find him and that was what was important. Warrior's face rose before her closed eyes. She thought of stroking his huge, powerful neck and holding that beautiful head in her hands. When she surfaced for air, her right side slammed into a boulder, which threw her sideways into an eddy, a pocket of still water between the rocks and the shore. Stunned, Sayre opened her eyes, turned over and floated in the water trying to decide if she was dead.

She opened and closed her eyes several times and determined that she must be alive. She gingerly raised her right arm and leg and discovered that they could move. Feeling more confident, she swam the short distance to shore and pulled herself onto the bank. She was trembling so severely that she couldn't stand, so she just lay still. She was overcome by exhaustion and shock, and had no idea how she could ever marshal the strength to seek the help she needed. For now, lying on dry ground was enough.

Suddenly she felt a wet nose nudge her face. Opening her eyes, she saw Lady and heard a familiar deep voice calling to her from the woods. Sayre immediately tried to sit up, but felt so dizzy that she collapsed again, comforted to know that Freeman was nearby. She was alive. She was safe.

When Freeman saw her, he yelled to several men behind

him, "He's here. Looks like the creek threw him out." Quietly, so that only she could hear, he continued gently, "Sayre, you all right?"

"Yes, I think so" she replied. "I just can't get up. I hit a rock and eddied out. Warrior must've been looking out for me. I saw him so clearly when I was under the water. I'm fine. Only... could you help me up? I think I can walk once I get upright."

Four black men emerged from the woods and stood silently by as Sayre tried her legs. Her stance was shaky, but she took a few short steps and remained upright.

"I can get back to the trail," she said in a voice that sounded to her as if she were talking from a distance.

"I'll walk back with you, see that you're settled. Then I've gotta go back out. We're walkin' the banks to look for survivors or..." Freeman's voice trailed off. "A lot of folks ended up in the water. Some made it, but others didn't. You can rest near Sally's brood and Lady'll be there too. I need to patch 'er up again."

He put his arm around Sayre and steadied her as they walked. The four men continued on downstream. One was carrying a shovel.

Chapter 15

The scene back at the pontoon bridge was chaos. Several men on the far side had fashioned a raft from abandoned wood and were ferrying people across into the arms of another group of men who had lined up to take them ashore from the raft. The Union Army had disappeared, leaving the devastated blacks to fend for themselves. Yet the people's desire to follow their liberators seemed unshaken.

Lady ran ahead and sat near the wagon. She barked when she saw Freeman and Sayre. Her wound had stopped bleeding and the blood had begun to dry on her forehead. Sayre desperately wanted to lie down under something warm and dry, and nuzzle next to Lady. She ached in every part of her body, particularly where she had hit the rock, but she was not about to complain. She was alive.

Back at the wagon, Sayre found her dry clothes and struggled awkwardly beneath a quilt to put them on. They felt warm and made her think of home. She made an attempt to drape her wet clothes over the side of the wagon and then snuggled down under the quilt. Hearing the pandemonium continuing at the creek, she wanted to go there, wanted to help, but could only whisper, "Thank you, Warrior. I know you were with me in that water." Then darkness enveloped her.

Sayre awoke to a cacophony surrounding her. She opened her eyes slowly and was immediately aware of pain. Every fiber of her body reverberated with it. Her head throbbed and she felt sick.

Best to just lie here, she thought. Freemen will come and make everything better.

She vaguely realized Lady was not beside her, probably at the campfire begging for morsels of food. It didn't matter. Sayre closed her eyes again. All that day she drifted in and out of sleep. At some point she heard Freeman's voice near her. Beauty, who must have been tethered close by, nickered softly, and Lady barked a welcome.

Finally, Sayre's head cleared enough to comprehend Freeman as he asked quietly, "Sayre, are you awake?"

She was able to reply, "Yes."

"Have you tried to get up?"

"It didn't work out too well. Are we safe? Is the baby alright?"

"Yes, little Jonah is fine. Later on, we'll talk. For now, you rest. We're still cleaning up the mess from last night. All up and down both sides of the creek, there are folks alive and folks dead. I'm going out with more men to do what we can."

As he began to move away from her, cramming a hat on his head and picking up a shovel, he said quietly to himself, " Never seen anyone act like those soldiers did. Didn't care about any of these people. Seems like President Lincoln's fine law don't mean much at times."

"Sayre," he called back to her, "You need anything, Sally's nearby. Her husband hasn't come back yet. Guess he's moving on with the army. Let's just hope the Confederates don't find us. We've heard some musket fire in the distance. When you've rested, I'll tell you my plan."

Sayre nodded and pulled the quilt tightly around her. She was too drained to understand fully. At this moment, she didn't care much about the danger. She closed her eyes, snuggled farther under the quilt, and began dreaming again of Warrior, the cabin, the woods.

When she opened her eyes, it was dark. Slowly she sat up. Her hand found Lady's side and she began to rub the dog gently. She felt better. Moving could still be a problem, she determined, so she began by wiggling her toes, then moving her legs. Pain shot through her body. Nevertheless, she took a slow breath, put the quilt aside, and crawled to the back of the wagon. So far, she was only slightly dizzy. Her leg and arm hurt, but that was to be expected. She carefully lowered herself to the ground, then walked toward the campfire. Sally sat with her children, rocking the rescued Jonah in her lap.

"Sayre," Sally greeted her. "Sit down. We've got some collard greens and pot liquor. It'll do you good. My Parsy brought it back from the army. He just rode in."

Sayre looked over to see a short, sturdy man, who nodded to her.

Sally continued. "Parsy's going to be here tonight, then head back up to help guide the army through the swamp. Guess we're heading to Savannah. Freeman should be back by now. He and four men have been gone since early this morning and only came back to check on you."

"Yes, I remember. Guess I slept all day."

"Sure did. You were dead tired, but you sure did save my baby, and for that I'm mighty grateful."

Parsy spoke up. "Son, that was a brave thing you did and I'll be the first to say it."

Sayre nodded, scooped the hot pot liquor into her mouth, loving its taste, warmth and healing powers. The greens were just as good and she quickly devoured them. Feeling well fed for the first time in many days, she sat next to the fire and stared into the flames. She heard people approaching. Parsy cocked his rifle and pointed it in the direction of the sounds.

"Parsy, it's just me," Freeman called as he and Lady came from the woods. "Sayre, I'm glad to see you up! Well, Sally, we're fixin' to add to your family right here, right now!"

With that, Freeman walked to the campfire. A broad smile lit his face and in his arms he carried a toddler.

"Here he is. We call him Moses, 'cause we found him in the bulrushes. Well, not exactly, but some mighty tall grass. Just sitting there where the creek had deposited him. No one around, not even bodies, although we did find plenty of them too. Buried everyone and said a prayer. At least they died free."

Parsy and Sally nodded, but they stared at the small child.

Freeman continued. "I gotta hope we might find his kinfolk, but, Sally, will you take him in at least for now? Sayre and I will help take care of him. He's a good boy. Only cried a little. Slept most of the way on my back."

The tiny child sneezed in his sleep, then nuzzled more closely to his rescuer. Freeman turned to Sayre and gave her one of the wide smiles that always made her grin in return.

"Reckon we can't refuse." Sally said. "Food's getting scarce, but maybe we'll make up for that with some attention and love. I figure he's maybe two, three years old."

Parsy nodded. "When I meet back up with the army, I'll spread the word. Maybe some family member's alive, and looking for the boy."

As Parsy took Jonah, Freeman handed Moses to Sally. The foundling stirred, his eyelids fluttered.

"Time for him to meet my other children," Sally said. She smiled at him as he opened his eyes. "You're a strong, healthy little thing, aren't you? Tomorrow, we'll look for your family, but for now, we'll settle you in with us."

Sally and Parsy moved to where their children were playing under a pine tree, and Freeman sat down next to Sayre. His tone was solemn. "Sayre. I've been thinkin'. We can't continue like this, and…"

Sayre jerked her head to look at him.

He raised his hand to stop her protest.

"Here's what I think," he continued. "My plan is we hook up with the Union Army directly. Work for them or somethin'. It's the only way we're gonna survive out here, caught between the Yankees and Wheeler's cavalry. The Confederates aren't going to let this army continue without some serious fightin'. You're good with horses. I'm the best blacksmith there is. I suspect the Yankee army could use us. Parsy can talk to the men he's working with and recommend us."

Sayre was already shaking her head. "You want me to help the Yankees?" She scowled at Freeman.

He pressed on. "This way we may have a better chance of finding Warrior; then we can hatch a new plan to get him home. But, I gotta tell you, right now I'm most concerned with keeping us alive. The way things are going, we'll be captured by the Confederates or the Union. One of them will pick us up or pick us off. I'm sure about that!"

Sayre sat silently. What a twist, she thought. Her papa was with one army, and now she was suddenly thinking about signing on with the other. However, with Freeman's plan there was the possibility of seeing and rescuing Warrior. She would have to ponder how to handle living around the Yankees. But she knew she could do it.

She turned to her friend. "Freeman," she said. "It's a sensible plan. Check with Parsy and see if he can help. Once you talk with him, we'll know if it would work."

CHAPTER 16

"*P*arsy," Freeman called. "I have a question to ask you. Actually, a favor, I guess."

Parsy paused as he put his foot in the stirrup and hoisted himself into the saddle. "What you need? If I can help, I will. Sayre saved my baby. I'd like to repay that debt, any way I can."

"Sally says you're head of a team clearing roads and cutting new ones for the army. Being a foreman on the plantation, you know how to handle workers. My guess is that makes you mighty important to Mr. Sherman and the Union soldiers."

"Oh, I don't know about that, but, yes, me and my men work alongside the white soldiers."

"Well, we really need to get to Savannah, and I figure the safest way to do that is to join the Union Army. Now, I'm a pretty good blacksmith and Sayre has a special way with horses. We'll both work hard. If you could help put in a good word for us, we'd be mighty obliged. We don't know if Sayre's pa is dead or alive, but right now it don't make any difference. My job is to get that boy to his kinfolk. Sure don't want the Confederates to stop us and send me to some plantation even though I got my papers."

"I'm afraid you may be right. I'm thinking of bringing Sally and the children into one of the camps behind the army for the same reason. Her and the children are accustomed to hard work. They can do most anything. Anyway, I'll see what I can do for you. The Yanks did ask me to find some more good workers for them. Stay near Sally and the children. That way it'll be easy to find you."

Freeman walked back to the wagon where Sayre was repacking their dwindling supplies. Beauty was harnessed, Lady sitting on the seat in her usual spot. When the last box was in place, Freeman grabbed the reins, clucked to Beauty, and eased the wagon to where Sally and the children were waiting to climb aboard. Sally was holding Moses. The foundling remained very quiet as if trying to figure out who these strangers were. Freeman clucked and the wagon joined the procession moving down the road.

Sayre looked over her shoulder at the still-swollen creek. She shuddered slightly and could still feel the water over her head, the loneliness of near death and the fight for simple air. She looked at Moses and marveled that one so small and calm had survived such an ordeal. His dark skin shone in the early morning light.

Where are you, Warrior? she thought. Do you know I'm coming to find you? I'm here, Warrior. I'm here. I'm coming, and if I have to join the Bluecoats to do it, that's what I'll do.

The band of blacks slowly moved forward down the road. There were now far fewer. Many had simply become discouraged and turned back to the only lives they knew.

Time passed slowly. The air became cold and damp. Freeman and Sayre had begun to ration their food even more carefully, and they kept a sharp eye toward each side of the road, hoping for opportunities to forage. Acorns they had collected along the way became a staple. Lady was surviving on beef jerky that Freeman and Sayre had packed for themselves in case hunting was poor. They'd never anticipated that traveling with so many others would leave the land stripped of wildlife, mile after mile.

They still encountered few inhabitants. The doors of the cabins that remained were shut tightly to newly freed slaves or anyone with them.

On the third day's journey from the creek, Parsy came riding down the road on a huge roan horse, not his usual mount. Sally was sitting in the front of the wagon with Freeman while Sayre and Lady took a turn in the back with the children. Moses was cradled in Sayre's arms, playing with a toy Freeman had fashioned from acorn shells. Sayre held him tightly, her head resting against his.

"Sally, good news! Freeman, pull over. Good news for us all," Parsy shouted as a wide grin filled his face.

Freeman slowed the wagon and Sayre poked her head out from the back in time to hear Parsy explain. "I had a chance to talk to the quartermaster, Captain Bradford. I'd just helped clear the road of what they call 'land mines'— these long copper cylinders that'll blow up if they're touched. The Confederates have planted a lot of them. Hurt a lot of people. But I've got sort of a knack for handling them and my willingness to pull the things apart earned me some good words. So I thought it would be a good time to ask for a favor."

Sally shifted her gaze into the distance, probably unhappy that her husband should have so perilous an occupation.

Parsy continued. "Anyway, Quartermaster Bradford introduced me to a lady by the name of Mrs. Hill and he put in a good word with her. Sally, I know for sure that you'll be helping Mrs. Hill. She runs the hospital that travels with the army. You and the children will have a tent, not large, but it'll mean a place to sleep and some food. Freeman, I can't promise nothing for you or Sayre, but Quartermaster Bradford asked Mrs. Hill to talk to you. If she approves of you, you can work, too."

Parsy's face clouded slightly. "I must say, Mrs. Hill is awfully…well, you'll see for yourself soon enough. You're all gonna follow me right now and we'll go talk to her. The army has slowed coming into Savannah. Sherman's trying to figure out what Hardee's gonna do, whether he'll stand and fight or try to get his army out of the city. Looks like the camp might be sitting awhile, so this is our chance."

"Thank you, Parsy," Sayre said. "Seems like there couldn't be a better time to join the Union Army."

They all laughed and Parsy looked fondly at his children. "Pretty soon you're gonna be working hard again, but the good news is we'll be together and safe."

Then he turned his horse and trotted down the road. Under Freeman's firm hand, Beauty stepped forward at a quicker pace, headed for what would be the safety of the conquering army. Sayre shifted Moses and repositioned herself so she could fasten her eyes on the road as the wagon rolled along the path, moving her closer to Warrior and all the unknowns that lay ahead.

Chapter 17

When Sayre thought about the army, any army, she thought about her papa. She had gotten through the years since his departure by imagining him safe and well. Still, her mental image of his life in the military was dominated by battles and marches. In recent months, she'd seen her fill of soldiers on the march, and she'd been steeling herself for the sight of actual battle. Instead, if she was accepted, she was to become a part of the support system that kept an army functioning.

With the bulk of the fighting force miles in the distance, Sayre and Freeman found themselves in the yard of an abandoned farmhouse that had been transformed into a field hospital. The nearby barn served as an infirmary-like stable for wounded horses, mainly those of the officers.

"Whoa, Beauty," Freeman said, and when the wagon stopped, he and Sayre stepped down beside it.

Surveying the travelers was a large woman clad in a black dress with a heavily starched white lace collar, her deep brown hair pulled tightly into a bun. Freeman held his hat in his hand. Sayre tried to look meek and respectful, her stomach knotting. Lady refused to stay in the wagon and now sat alertly at their feet.

Parsy stood behind them, twirling his hat in his hand as he spoke, "These are the two I told Captain Bradford about, ma'am."

"Yes. So you are Freeman, a blacksmith. And you are Sayre, an orphan from Georgia. A Southerner." The woman's piercing gaze fixed on Sayre, who did not dare meet her eyes.

Mrs. Hill shifted her focus to Freeman. "Because our blacksmith must now ride with the troops, we can certainly use your skills here, Freeman. And if, as Parsy tells us, you have a way with horses, then you are doubly welcome. Our cavalry is engaged in a great number of skirmishes with Wheeler's cavalry, and we have many horses coming from the front in need of care. No fresh animals have come from Washington, though we've heard there are a great many there."

Mrs.Hill turned again to Sayre. "Parsy says you are educated?"

"Yes, ma'am. My papa taught me to read and write."

Surely her literacy was an asset, but Sayre suddenly worried that it could seem suspicious to Mrs. Hill. It was hard to tell what was important to these people. Sayre grew increasingly anxious. If this plan didn't work, what chance did they have?

"As for this dog," Mrs. Hill began.

"She's mine," Freeman interjected. "Rescued her. She's no bother. She'll stay with me. She's a good guard dog so she'll protect the tools in the smithy. I can keep her in the stable area."

"And I can sleep anywhere," Sayre offered. "The stable would be fine for me too. I've slept in stalls and sheds along the way." She knew she must sound desperate as she blurted out, "And we don't eat much."

"I see," Mrs. Hill mused. "You aren't afraid of hard work?"

"No, ma'am, not at all. I can do whatever you need. I even like mucking stalls," Sayre replied. "I love everything about horses. My papa said the way you can tell someone is a horse person is when he walks into a stable and smells the odor and thinks it smells like perfume. I just like caring for horses. I mean, if that's what you need me to do..."

Sayre fell silent, fearing she had talked too much.

Mrs. Hill looked at them, carefully scrutinizing each one. There were spies within the Union Army, she knew, spies who looked and acted innocent enough.

Finally, she spoke. "I will make my report to Captain Bradford. Freeman, I'd like you to begin at once in the smithy. It's there at the barn. I have nothing to do with horses or blacksmiths, but they and we do travel together. Sayre, you will be here on probation. If the quartermaster is pleased, then you may stay too."

"Thank you," Freeman said and Sayre echoed his words.

"Now, I must tell you that I run a tight ship. I took over command of this medical unit from Mrs. Bickerdyke when she left after the Battle of Atlanta. An amazing woman. Even General Sherman stayed out of her way. She'd put together a nomadic hospital to follow the troops and care for the wounded back when the army left Illinois. Parsy's family will be rolling bandages and helping to make these dear brave boys more comfortable."

Her stern face almost softened before she pressed on. "At any time, if your dog causes trouble, she goes. You both could go with her. You will need to make yourselves useful and keep out of trouble. Any questions?"

Silence.

"Good. Freeman, please find a place in the stable to bunk. Sayre, there's a small spot in the hospital for you. You will follow me."

With that Mrs. Hill turned and strode with purpose toward the spacious farmhouse. Glancing at Freeman in barely disguised panic, Sayre followed, hoping her gait was convincingly masculine.

When she saw that the space was a storage shed behind the kitchen, Sayre concurred with the description "small," but that didn't trouble her. With so few belongings, it took very little space to feel comfortable. The small cot, with its thin cotton sheet and lumpy pillow, was certainly better than the ground or the back of the wagon where she had slept of late.

Sayre went back to the wagon and retrieved a quilt, the brown carpetbag containing her clothes, her box of feathers and the hair from Warrior's mane, her fiddle, and the precious book of Shakespeare. She carefully set these treasures on the ground next to the cot and wondered how long this sparse corner would be her home.

This task finished, Sayre hurried back to find Freeman. He was in a makeshift stall, and Beauty munched on hay nearby. Lady was stretched out sound asleep. The dog stirred when Sayre approached, but could only muster a sigh before dozing off again. Her wound was healing well, but there would certainly be a nagging scar to remind her caretakers of this war and her close call with death.

Freeman was busily inspecting the traveling forge that shared space with the animals. "Seems pretty fit, Sayre. The only thing I'll need to do is rebuild a section of the coal box. The bellows are worn but workable, and there are maybe a hundred pairs of horseshoes and thirty pounds of nails here. Whoever stocks the supplies is doing a good job."

"There's a pen outside," Sayre said, "for the horses that come in. I passed it when I was looking for you. Since I'm not sure what I'm supposed to be doing right now, I reckon I'd better help you. I certainly don't want Mrs. Hill to find me idle."

The two shared a smile and began opening trunks of brushes, hoof picks, combs, bits, leather for repairing saddles, reins, or halters, and saddle soap and oil for cleaning and preserving the tack.

Freeman shook his head. "This army was well supplied. I bet the other side's got nothing like this, especially now that Sherman's destroyed so many factories in Georgia. To me, that means this war can't last much longer."

Sayre looked up at him. "You might be right, and I have to say I hope it's over and done with soon. We've only seen a small piece of this war and it's more terrible than I could have imagined. Win or lose," she said, "I want it over, but from what I've seen, no one will really win. The country has been torn apart, and it'll take a long time to heal."

Then she returned to inspecting the trunks, memorizing the location of each item that would be needed. Sayre thought of Warrior and the countless times her hands had brushed his coat to a shining gloss, combed his mane and tail, picked his hooves, cleaned his ears, then fed him a carrot or two and an apple if they had one, for good measure. As she opened yet another trunk, her mind wandered back to his pasture, the creek, and the last time she'd touched him.

She was so far away in her reverie that Mrs. Hill's voice startled her. "Sayre, you are needed rolling bandages with Sally and her children. Follow me. No horses today."

"Yes, ma'am," Sayre said. "Bandages."

CHAPTER 18

*N*ews came that Confederate General Hardee had escaped across the Savannah River into South Carolina. Under cover of fog, the ragtag Confederate Army of nine thousand infantry, a few artillerymen, cannons, and baggage wagons had vanished. It was December 20, 1864, only one month since the Yankees had marched past Sayre's farm. True to his word, Sherman had marched to the sea in record time and now the general presented the vanquished city of Savannah as a Christmas gift to President Lincoln.

Although Savannah had fallen without a major battle, the opposing armies were now so close to each other that minor skirmishes developed throughout the area. Wheeler's cavalry and Kilpatrick's cavalry sparred daily, and almost immediately wounded men and horses had to be evacuated from the front to receive urgent care. Sally and her children were ably producing bandages, so Sayre was reassigned to assist with the horses.

Some of the animals that began arriving were terribly jaded, ridden almost to death; others suffered from various illnesses. Sayre began her task of nursing them back to health with lots of hay, a strict diet of grain, and her special brand of love. She brushed them two or three times a day and talked to them incessantly, hoping to bring back their spirit. She could look at their eyes and know what they were feeling, especially those that seemed to have given up all interest in life, the ones with dead eyes. Sayre's remedy for them was more attention, more soft words.

Hoof rot, grease heel, colic, and deep scratches from riding through thick underbrush were common ailments, and Freeman moved from blacksmithing to horse doctoring. He was particularly good with colic cases which were usually a result of overwork, too much water, or bad grain. Sayre remembered her father talking about a horse's stomach and what a delicate organ it is, quite primitive for so large an animal. Over the centuries, the horse's digestive system had not kept up with the refinements of its body, and so it broke down easily, particularly under harsh conditions.

In severe cases, Freeman administered mineral oil and Sayre walked the animal so it would not lie down, which could twist its intestines, causing a painful death. On many nights, the kerosene lantern burned well into the early morning as they took turns guiding sick animals around the corral until their discomfort eased and the danger of losing them lessened.

Even though the main Confederate army had disappeared, Sherman was more than content to hold the port city, burn its twenty five thousand bales of cotton, and orchestrate the capture of one of the country's most significant regions. He began making plans to invade South Carolina, his real target, in order to punish its inhabitants for leading the way into secession. In the short term, his road-weary army needed time to rest.

In between patients, Sayre also cleaned and oiled saddles. The Union Army rode a style designed before the war by George McClellan: a cross between a western and English saddle, and a very comfortable ride. Observing the horses sent behind the lines to recover also revealed other preferences in tack. She saw that officers' horses had brass-plated steel bits. Although most of them were curved, Sayre was glad to see that a few snaffles appeared now and then. Because it was lighter and less severe than a curved bit, Sayre had always used a snaffle on Warrior. Papa had insisted.

Enjoying the mindless work, Sayre washed each piece of tack with saddle soap, then rubbed it with oil until it glowed. She loved how it looked, felt, and smelled when she finished. Sometimes, cavalry officers coming to retrieve their recuperated horses would ask her to shine their boots and she willingly agreed- anything to make a good impression that would allow her to stay and wait.

Word spread of the skillful new hands at the stable and their success with the horses. Mrs. Hill confirmed this impression when she appeared early one day. Sayre was cleaning a saddle, Freeman shoeing a horse. Lady was sitting quietly on the ground just outside the stable.

"Freeman," Mrs. Hill said as she approached the smithy. "I'm coming to report my morning conversation with Quartermaster Bradford. You and Sayre seem to be making a name for yourselves with the work you've been doing here. I hope you will continue with us. Both of you. We have some stiff fighting ahead before we conquer the Confederates and we need every horse we can muster."

Sayre's stomach tightened at the word "conquer" but she sat very still, her hand poised over the saddle.

"Yes, ma'am, we'll gladly continue," Freeman replied, looking at Sayre.

"Thank you," Sayre added, her eyes fastened on the saddle.

"Then be prepared to get underway within a few days," Mrs. Hill answered as she turned away. "General Sherman is heading into South Carolina."

Chapter 19

$\mathcal{T}$he camp was abuzz with excitement because the troops were once again preparing for battle. Sherman was to enter South Carolina on two fronts: Howard's wing had left Beaufort and was moving north. Fifty miles to the south in the deadly swamps, Slocum's men, following the Savannah River, were to eventually turn north and parallel Howard's army for their entrance into South Carolina's capital, Columbia.

For the first time, Freeman and Sayre experienced an army gearing up for a major offensive. From within this immense war machine on the move, Sayre could not forget that all the energy that hummed around her was aimed against people who fought on the same side as her father.

Soldiers and black volunteers appeared from nowhere to break down the corrals and stalls and load the tack into wagons. All of the hospital equipment, cots, and linens were stowed in trunks and loaded onto other wagons. Wounded men were moved to horse-drawn ambulances. Through it all, the rains were unrelenting and, by the time everything was ready, it was February 1, 1865. For reasons nobody at the rear of the army knew, Savannah had been spared the torch.

Freeman and Sayre loaded their small wagon and put Lady on the front seat. The horses still recovering under their care were tied to their wagon and to other wagons behind them. The march would be hard for these weakened animals, but they would be well cared for along the way. Parsy was driving a supply wagon and his family rode with him. If the army called Parsy to the front, Sally could easily take over the driving.

Holding Moses in her lap, Sayre rested her arm on Lady's back and gently stroked her head. The toddler followed suit, moving his tiny hand over the animal's fur. Lady had become a favorite in the camp. Lulled by the motion of the wagon, the girl considered how Lady had become part of so many lives. Since she rarely barked, the dog didn't disturb the recovering wounded, and whenever she did bark or growl, the camp was immediately alerted to the approach of a stranger.

Most of the time the dog stayed near the stable with Freeman and Sayre, but she sometimes accompanied soldiers who were able to walk around the camp as part of their recuperation. "Reminds me of my dog back home," was a frequent remark as Lady made friends with the patients. She would trot beside the soldier keeping pace with either a slow hobble or a strong walk.

Lady loved this attention, but she always returned in the evenings and sat beside Sayre as she began reading aloud from one of Shakespeare's plays. The book saw frequent use, but Sayre could not yet pick up her father's fiddle. She could muster no enthusiasm for bowing the strings. The instrument reminded her of home and gentler, happier times. For now, she was merely surviving and she was grateful for Lady's companionship.

Within days, the hospital wagons were moving through the streets of Savannah, where many windows were shuttered as if to keep out a storm. Few people were on the streets. Most of those who were visible were blacks, positioned to cheer the Union on to victory. There was no sign of the Confederates neither cavalry nor infantry.

When they were on the outskirts of the city, Freeman turned to Sayre and said in a low voice, " Keep your eyes on the road. Don't look right or left. The killing pens are ahead. Parsy warned me there were some around here."

"Killing pens?" she asked keeping her head down, as her hand felt for Lady's soft fur.

"Yes." Freeman replied. "That's the reason we haven't seen as many horses lately: a lot are considered no good anymore. Besides I've heard the Yankees have plenty in Washington ready to send down to end this war, so now they're rounding up the ones that's been used up. Fact is, they put them in a pen and shoot them."

Sayre raised her head and looked him in the eye, then spoke in a voice she could hardly recognize as her own. "Then we'll have to see if Warrior is in one of them." She took a deep breath. "How can we manage that without causing a stir?"

"Don't know; I was afraid you'd suggest that. Let me run back and talk to Parsy. At least we're at the rear. But, Sayre, we gotta keep up with the army and not fall so far behind that we become easy game for Confederates. And we can't let Mrs. Hill or Captain Bradford think we're too slow. I'm thinkin' maybe we can stop the wagons that have the sickest horses if we need to. That'll give me time to check the pens. But I don't think Warrior'll be there. He's too valuable."

"Yes he's valuable, but he might still have been hurt and..." Sayre stopped her words, stopped her thoughts, and deliberately returned to Freeman's proposed plan. "That's good thinking. It's our responsibility to feed and look after our horses, make them more comfortable, make sure they're okay. We surely can stop for that. And while that's going on, we can check the pens."

Freeman silently noticed that her final phrase had changed his "me" to "we."

"Sounds about right," he agreed, bringing Beauty to a halt at the side of the road.

He leapt from the wagon and jogged back to Parsy. Sayre sat still, not daring to look ahead. Her stomach churned. She clenched her jaw and swallowed hard.

In a few minutes, Freeman was back. "Parsy has two men who're going to untie the sick horses. They'll walk them around and water them, which'll give us time to look at both pens. Parsy reckons about fifty horses are in the pens. They're mighty big pens. I'll go look on my own, if you want." But he knew the answer.

Without a word, Sayre slid from the wagon, and pulled her hat down on her head. She could sense the unease in the horses she cared for. They whinnied softly as the smell of death reached their nostrils.

"Lady, stay," Sayre said. "We'll be back. This is not a place you need to go."

The large dog quietly lay down on the wagon seat, her sharp, dark eyes following Freeman and Sayre.

As they walked closer, the odor of decaying flesh was almost overpowering. Sayre gripped Freeman's arm and stared only at the road directly in front of the toes of her boots.

They reached the pens and Sayre climbed onto the rough fence looking at the bodies strewn inside. In nature, horses are prey animals and their instinct is to flee when sensing danger. These animals had sensed danger all around them as men had yelled and their rifles had blared. The horses' now-still eyes were wide, their nostrils flared and, though hours had passed since the slaughter, sweat still stood on their bodies, mute testament to how hard they'd run to avoid the bullets that had poured into their midst. Their deaths had not been easy or quick.

Sayre was sickened at the carnage. These beautiful animals had given so much. This was not the end they deserved. At least they'd have had honor if they had died in battle. There was no honor here. Summoning more courage than she knew she had, she began picking her way through the bodies, looking for that familiar chestnut head, his mane lying limp over the powerful neck, the bold eyes that would now be stilled. But Warrior was not here, nor was he in the pens on the other side of the road.

Sayre turned from the sadness that hung in the air and walked slowly back to the wagon, Freeman silent at her side. The men had finished tending to the horses, and Freeman gave a signal to Parsy, which was repeated down the line. The wagons and their skittish herd began to move forward.

"I think I'll walk awhile if you don't mind," Sayre said.

"That'll be fine," Freeman murmured as Lady jumped down to trot beside the girl.

Sayre pushed her hat even further down on her head; then, just as she passed the last killing pen, she stopped. Had she heard a tiny whinny? Or was her mind playing tricks? Turning, she walked to the pen and listened. There it was again: a small sound skittered up from the silence. Ducking under the rails, she made her way once again through the dead horses. She was now watching for movement, for some flicker of life. Freeman was quickly beside her, and both began moving in a circle. Yes, there it was again. A tiny sound. Two other men had come inside and they, too, were combing through the bodies.

One shouted, "Over here! He's over here," and everyone ran to the spot where the man pointed.

A dark bay lay still, blood streaking his shoulders and face. But his eyes moved and he was breathing. A dead horse's legs had pinned him to the ground, and he wasn't attempting to get up, only making sounds as if to protest the grotesque insanity around him.

As Freeman and the two men maneuvered the body of the slain horse away from the trapped animal, the bay struggled to stand. Freeman had a rope at the ready and he tied it around the horse's neck.

"Stand back," he called. "When he gets up, no telling what he'll do."

Sayre backed away, but began talking in soothing tones.

"Whoa, fella. Good boy. Whoa! There, you've almost made it. Steady. No one will hurt you. It's all over. Whoa! Good boy! Good boy!"

The animal's eyes were white with fear, but he didn't fight. Finally, when he was standing, he looked around and snorted.

One of the men pulled two rough wooden rails from the side of the pen so Freeman could lead the injured horse through the opening. The horse was nickering softly, small staccato sounds as if trying to make sense of what had happened-what was happening now. His ears flicked from side to side.

Sayre held the rails back as the animal emerged; then she ran to the wagon and brought a cloth to wipe away the blood so she could assess how serious the wound might be. This was not Warrior, but it was an animal in need of her care.

He was a big horse, at least 15.3 hands, painfully thin, and Sayre noticed that when he walked, he limped. He'd sustained two wounds: one bullet must have grazed his skull and another had grazed his shoulder. They had caused him to fall, and he had then been left for dead.

Freeman stepped beside Sayre with a bucket of water and a cloth and began rubbing the horse down. As the water and soothing hands touched him, the bay began to shake. Small shudders ran throughout his body. Sayre massaged his face. She cooed soft words to him as Freeman worked on the wounds. Gradually, the shudders stopped and the animal stood still, his head down.

"I'll walk with him," Sayre said, "if he can make it."

"We'll see if he can. Don't get your hopes up, Sayre."

Sayre held the rope and whispered to the horse, "Come on, my brave soldier. Let's head north."

Chapter 20

"Salkehatchie," Freeman mused as he drove the last post of a new corral into the ground. "Salkehatchie – name beats all. We've heard some good ones on this trip, Sayre. Maybe not the best way to see the country, but we're hitting small towns and big ones. I'm glad we're stopping for a while. Parsy says there was a big fight at the river called Salkehatchie. Seems the Confederates had a bunch of men lying in wait for Sherman's troops. Apparently, old Joe Mower was the Southern commander. So, how's that poor horse doing, Sayre?"

"His limp's almost gone and the wounds are healing, thanks to your brown wormwood. Only thing really worries me are his eyes. They show he's still scared, but I can't talk him out of it. I tried reading him *A Midsummer Night's Dream* last night, but that didn't work either."

Sayre finished brushing the wounded bay they had rescued from the killing pens. Once again she took his head in her hands, blew in his nostrils, and used her fingers to draw circles around his eyes, the special technique she had been using each day to calm the horse and reassure him that he was finally safe or as safe as she and Freeman could make him in this violent world which surrounded them. She had walked him all the way here to their new hospital and stable, leading him gently beside the wagon. Now with news of serious skirmishes with the Confederates, she and Freeman anticipated more wounded horses and men.

Temporary facilities for both were being thrown up far behind the Union lines. Under Mrs. Hill's watchful eye, the soldiers commandeered another farmhouse with a huge barn. They would be here a couple of weeks, long enough for the fighters—both human and animal—to mend or to die. Sayre helped remove the heavy boxes of stable supplies from the wagons and sorted through them again to make sure she was ready for her work ahead. Meanwhile, Freeman and the men were quickly fencing a corral and arranging separate stalls for the most critical cases.

In the past two days, Freeman had managed to add a young goat to their menagerie. One of the men had found the scrawny creature in a ravine near the road. Presumably having strayed too far from its pasture, the goat had been grazed by a bullet and then must have tumbled down a hillside into the swampy land below. Trapped in the deep, sticky mud, she'd mustered the strength to bleat forcefully, calling attention to her plight.

Since meat was a rare treat, goat was immediately put on the camp's menu, but Freeman had intervened, explaining that he needed the goat as a companion for his ailing horses.

"Horses are mighty social animals," he'd told the incredulous man. "They need their herd. For some of our horses, this goat will be the ticket back to good health. You just watch and see."

The man had relinquished his prize reluctantly, and Freeman had named the goat "Gracie," alluding to the grace displayed in allowing her to live.

Sayre and Lady warmed to her immediately, but Gracie only followed Freeman. At his command, she would stay in a corral with a horse, instantly calming the larger animal. This boon notwithstanding, Mrs. Hill looked on Gracie with disdain, and Gracie, in turn, avoided the woman whenever possible.

Luckily, Mrs. Hill was busy preparing her latest makeshift hospital. Sally and her offspring were rolling more bandages and handling the washing. Moses had become a special part of the family and was perfectly comfortable with any of the children, but particularly loved being around Sayre. When Parsy was around, Moses was inevitably riding on the man's shoulders and grinning broadly. If Sayre had a moment, she held him in her lap and read to him, sharing the bond forged in Ebenezer Creek.

Part of Sherman's army was now headed to Barnwell, South Carolina. It seemed that in this part of its territory, the South had nothing of consequence to stop the advance of this determined general. Elsewhere, the Confederacy might still be mounting a substantial defense, but here there was only a succession of small skirmishes. Still, it was enough to send wounded men to the field hospital.

Sayre contented herself temporarily with the rescued horse they now called Magic because he had magically out-smarted death. Although there had been more than one hundred dead horses and mules when they'd saved this one horse, saving even one life in this war was reassuring.

Sayre leaned down to pet Lady. "Hmm," she mused, "you were number one, then there was Moses and Magic, that's two and three, and Gracie makes four."

The numbers were adding up, but the one she most wanted to rescue from all this was still eluding her. She knew he was out there somewhere.

The sound of many hoofbeats broke her reverie. She put Magic in one of the makeshift stalls, gave him hay to munch on, and walked out to the new corral. As she did, four riders leading seven horses rode past her and stopped near Freeman.

"I'm Sergeant Sparling. The lieutenant back there told me to find a Freeman. These are officers' horses wounded in the skirmish with Hardee's men. We're specifically to find this Freeman fellow. Says they want only the best to mend these animals. Know where I can find him?"

"Yes, sir," Freeman responded with a twinkle in his eye. "Pretty close to here. I'll take them. I'm Freeman. This is my young friend, Sayre. He'll help get them settled in."

Freeman moved closer to one of the horses and began to examine a particularly nasty wound in the animal's chest, "Seems like they've had some attention already," he continued as Sayre stepped up to take the reins from the soldiers.

"You got a real animal doctor around here?" the sergeant asked, looking suspiciously at this black man and teenage boy. "You sure you know what you're doing? I'm not complaining, just asking."

"Well," Freeman said, the same twinkle in his eye. "We've had pretty good success so far. Just leave 'em with us. Where you headed?"

"Barnwell. Once we get through with it, it'll need to be called 'Burnwell.' We're aiming to destroy as much as we can in South Carolina. But all you need to know is that an orderly is bringing Captain Henry's horse to you. Should be along pretty soon. The captain's been wounded pretty badly and couldn't be moved. Amazingly his mount survived. Don't know when he'll be here. There's a lot of confusion near the front."

With that the four men turned their horses and rode off, leaving the seven wounded animals behind.

"Well, let's get busy, Sayre. Looks like we got our work cut out for us tonight. Let's get them settled and we can look at the wounds, then take the worst one first. I'm gonna need a lot of wormwood. This poor horse here looks to have glanders and hasn't been wounded at all. See those lesions with the pus on his flanks?"

"Sure do. I'll take him and start brewing up a mixture to put in his feed. Then I'll come help with the others."

Freeman called to the men finishing the corral. "When you're done, you can give us a hand with these animals. The horses came quicker than we expected."

Even with the additional hands, it was well past midnight when the last horse had been treated, fed, and made as comfortable as the wounds allowed. Tired though she was, Sayre went to Magic's stall and began rubbing him down with a sponge and warm water, another way to calm him down. She yearned to sleep, just to pull the covers over her head. When she finished, she went to Freeman who was still washing out a deep leg wound on a particularly beautiful gray mare.

"Mind if I turn in?" she asked.

"Nope. This one'll do it for me. Think we're on our way with these, but I have a feelin' more'll be comin' tomorrow."

"Then I'm going to bed. I'll be up early to check on them all. Magic is tucked in for the night. Mind if I take Lady with me? I'd like the company and sometimes she'll condescend to sleep by my cot."

"Nope. Don't mind at all." and Freeman chuckled as he nudged Lady to follow Sayre. "Gracie'll keep me company, won't you, little one?" His hand found the head of the animal and he rubbed it gently. Gracie, glad for the attention, moved closer to Freeman.

The air was chilly and damp, and Sayre pulled her coat tighter around her body. This brought to mind a certain new problem: her breasts. They had grown enough to worry her. Until now, she had been able to conceal them with layers of shirts, jackets, whatever she could come up with, but her shape was becoming more pronounced. As this was not the time to break her disguise, she would have to think of some way to bind her chest, especially as the weather grew warmer and she needed to wear fewer garments. Sayre resolved to ponder this in the morning. Right now, her body ached from the day's hard work. She took off her coat, hat, and boots, blew out the lamp, and slid under the sheet on the cot in the hospital ,Lady on the dirt beside her, and she fell into a deep and dreamless sleep quickly.

Shouting startled them awake and Lady growled. There were men's voices everywhere. Somewhere there was the sound of a horse galloping. Sayre was too dazed to make much sense of the situation, so she threw on her coat and hat, slid her feet into her boots, and ran toward the stable with Lady by her side.

More shouting, more hoofbeats, frantic whinnies. She rounded the corner of the stable and literally ran into Parsy.

"What's going on? What's happening? Where's Freeman?"

"Sayre, there's a wounded horse. The orderly brought him in, but he broke loose. Freeman got him into the corral, but the poor animal won't stop running, and he's bleeding pretty bad. Stay back. He's wild!"

Sayre didn't heed that warning. She was frightened for Freeman.

"Lady, stay here," she commanded, and the dog lay down next to Parsy, who was not venturing toward the terrified, dangerous animal.

Sayre walked quickly to where Freeman was standing outside the corral as the horse bolted from side to side. Blood and sweat coated his flanks; his eyes were wide and nearly white, his nostrils flared. He kicked out at whatever demon was pursuing him, then bucked and ran again.

Sayre stared at the animal, then looked at Freeman, who turned and nodded. Slowly, Sayre climbed onto the railing and cooed.

"Good boy. Good boy." She whistled softly, a gentle song that filled the night air.

The horse stopped, but only for a second, then resumed hurtling frantically around the enclosure. More blood mixed with sweat sprayed from his body. Fear and pain showed in his face.

"Good boy," Sayre said even more gently, tears streaming from her eyes. "You are a good boy!"

This time the dazed animal stopped, pawed the ground, and tossed his head high, captivated by the voice coming through the still, cool air, a voice he seemed to recognize. His ears pitched forward as again he heard the familiar sound. He pranced from side to side, whinnied, then stood still. Sayre carefully descended into the circle and walked toward him. When she was near him, she whispered the one word she had so longed to say, "Warrior."

Chapter 21

reeman called to the other men who had come to help, "Thanks. We got him now. He's ours for the night. Go on back to sleep, and thanks again."

Sayre slipped a halter over Warrior's head. She could not stop crying, and when she looked at Freeman, he was dabbing at his eyes with a well-worn handkerchief. He handed Sayre a lead rope and she fastened it to the halter and led Warrior to a stall where she and Freeman could better assess his wounds. The battle must have been ferocious. Warrior had been shot through the neck and had a deep saber gash on his flank. There were cuts all over his legs.

Their first job was to wash the wounds. Next, Freeman meticulously applied wormwood ointment to the raw flesh while Sayre continued to rub down Warrior's body, all the time talking to him in a hushed voice. She placed fresh hay in the stall, brought water, and gave him some corn feed. She was glad to see that his appetite was good. She was thankful he was with her, thankful he was alive.

When Warrior was as comfortable as they could make him, Freeman said, "It's almost morning. You go back and sleep a little longer. Warrior needs the rest too. I don't think those wounds will fester, but he's hurt pretty bad. Go on now so he can settle. Lady, Gracie, and I'll be nearby."

The girl did not budge.

"Sayre, if you work yourself to death, you'll be no good to Warrior. This ain't over yet, you know. My guess is we got a long way to go before we all make it back home."

Knowing that Freeman was right, Sayre reluctantly left his side.

She fell asleep almost immediately and didn't wake until close to noon. Parsy's little girl, Olivia, was at the side of her cot staring down at her. She held Moses by the hand. Sayre opened her eyes and smiled.

"Mama said you was tired and sent me to see if you was all right. Said you was up all night tending to the horses."

Sayre sat up and began putting on her boots. "Sure was, Olivia. Good morning,Moses," and she held out her hand for him to hold. "Have you two seen Freeman?"

"Sure have," Olivia said. "He's with the new horse. Said to let you sleep. I like that big new horse. He's pretty slashed up though. And they brought in a few more this morning. Had to put one down."

Sayre's hands clenched at the thought of another horse lost. She and Freeman were trying so hard to save them, but the odds had too often been in death's favor.

Her voice was low when she answered Olivia. "You're right about the new horse. He is beautiful and he's been in a bad fight." Sayre stood and shoved her hat on her head, then picked up Moses. "Come on. Let's go help Freeman."

Olivia put her small hand into Sayre's and they walked out to the stable. Freeman had a crew of men including Parsy now helping with the additional horses that had filled the little stable.

Word was coming in from the front that the Union Army had taken Columbia and was moving north. They had looted the city and destroyed most of the houses while the citizens fled into the countryside. With that conquest achieved, it was rumored that this hospital and stable, along with the nearby troops, would be moving in two weeks.

Two weeks, Sayre thought. In two weeks what will happen to Warrior? And then she put that thought out of her mind. I'll not think ahead. Now is what matters, she reminded herself. There's nothing I can do anyway but make him well and love him. It's a pure miracle he's here. In the whole war, he came to me. Papa, she thought, wherever you are, know that I am well. And then she smiled, although right now we're on opposite sides!

There was a steady bustle of activity around the injured animals. Gracie was in a small makeshift pen with a young gray thoroughbred gelding. Both were eating hay, the goat bleating in between mouthfuls of the rich grass. Freeman was there too, busily putting his special ointment on the gashes that covered the horse's body.

Other horses, whose recovery was further along, were grouped in the paddock. Sayre checked on the more serious cases in the stalls to see what they needed and what her tasks for the day would be.

She saved Warrior for last, but whenever she looked up, his massive head was sticking out of the stall to watch her every movement. To see him looking alert buoyed Sayre's spirit. At last, she walked to him, took his head in her hands and kissed his muzzle. Untying the ropes that served as a door, she walked into his stall and checked his wounds. They were deep but had stopped bleeding. Sayre went to get a halter and lead rope to walk him around a bit. Warrior seemed stiff, but followed her willingly. It was chilly and she stopped to fasten an oilcloth coat on him, making sure the pressure was not too great on his wounds. She could not believe she was leading Warrior. It had all happened so fast and her joy was complete. Nothing else mattered. He was here. He was hers once again.

As the days wore on, Warrior began to regain his strength, and Sayre opted to sleep in the stable to be near him. It was a simple matter since she only had a bedroll. Lady and Gracie slept nearby, and Freeman saw no reason to object.

Meanwhile, Magic was recovering nicely in the paddock, and a bit of the fear had gone from his eyes. Sayre washed and massaged all the horses, talked to them, mucked the stalls, and cleaned the paddocks. She and Freeman inventoried the supplies and requested more from Mrs. Hill when necessary. In contrast to what they'd heard about the poorly supplied Southern forces, the Union Army seemed well funded.

Within two weeks, most of their four-legged charges were able to return to their units. A few had perished. Too many soldiers didn't know how to care for their animals or believed in only "bleeding, blistering, or burning" to cure all ailments. When that didn't succeed, they might send the ailing animals behind the lines to people like Freeman and Sayre, who had to begin their work by undoing treatments that had proven more harmful than helpful.

Nine days after Warrior arrived, Sayre looked at his injuries and knew he was recovering well. She carefully put a bridle on his head and led him to Freeman.

"If you give me a leg up, we'll walk around the corral. No horses are there right now, and I think he can carry me."

"Be glad to," Freeman said, grinning. "Oh, and I have something for you. Found it this morning when we were repairing the fence line."

He pulled a beautiful azure feather from his pocket and handed it to Sayre.

"Blue jay," she said, and tucked it into her shirt pocket. "Thank you."

The black man cupped his hands and Sayre stepped into them, threw her right leg over Warrior's back, and grasped the reins. She clucked to him and felt the muscles in his back move as he walked to the corral. The feeling was pure magic. The power of his stride, the warmth of his skin, the view of the world as framed by his ears was what she had longed for. This time she didn't trot or canter. He wasn't ready for that yet, so they just walked. The small moment astride her beloved horse was going to be enough to take her through her long day and into the night. Whatever hard work lay ahead would have no chance to tarnish her joy.

After an hour, stopping often to let Warrior rest, Sayre slid to the ground and took him back to his stall. She rubbed him down vigorously with a damp sponge to increase his circulation, then cleaned his wounds again and applied more of the wormwood ointment. Then she mucked his stall, fed and watered him and then began working with the other animals.

As she left, Sayre kissed Warrior again and whispered, "I'll be back, and tonight we'll continue reading. I think Magic likes that too, and it's fun to laugh at characters Shakespeare created so long ago. I only wish Papa were here to laugh with us, but he will be someday, Warrior, just you wait and see."

Miles away from this tiny hospital, Sherman's army relentlessly marched through South Carolina, burning entire towns, destroying livestock and crops in a lurid celebration of triumph over the South. The North was invincible. Only Wheeler's cavalry, following on the heels of the Confederates' rear guard, kept a few towns from being destroyed. Still, their efforts were no match for the well-supplied and battle-hardened army heading now for North Carolina and Virginia and General Lee.

In the midst of this juggernaut, a young captain was anxious to return to Kilpatrick's cavalry, anxious to help reclaim the promise of a truly united United States. He was tired of the war, the senseless killing, but he believed in the goal and he had a job to do. He missed the horse he had grown to love and admire. The animal was smart in battle and more courageous than any mount he had ever ridden, and he was stunningly beautiful. His orderly had assured him that the animal's wounds were healing nicely. In a few days it would be time to send for him. They would be a team again. The young man stood and began to pace around the tent, tentatively at first. He could feel his own body becoming strong again, healing from the bullet wounds.

CHAPTER 22

"**J**ust give us a few minutes," Freeman said to the orderly. "Why don't you go up to the hospital? Maybe Mrs. Hill will have Sally fix you and your men a good breakfast. I know you've been riding hard. We'll get the captain's horse ready for the trip back. Sayre's with him now."

"Good. That horse is all the captain can talk about. He says he's ready to fight his way into Virginia if that's what it takes. Here, he sent this." The orderly handed over a handsome blanket. "Put it on him. The weather just won't warm up and I don't want to bring back a sick horse."

"The horse is mending well. Him and Sayre have bonded pretty good. That boy'll be sorry to see him go. And I hope you'll tell the captain to be sure and give the horse a couple more weeks before any serious riding."

"No need to worry there. I reckon he and the captain'll be ready to fight at about the same time. The captain sends his thanks. You know, you and that boy have quite a reputation in this army for tending to horses."

"Thank you," Freeman said with a nod. "We are a good team. Now, I hope you'll go ask Mrs. Hill about that breakfast and give the other men a rest. I'll get the horse ready."

When the orderly had gone, Freeman heaved a sigh and walked into the stable. Sayre was mucking Magic's stall, as Warrior stood in his stall nibbling on a few carrots that Sayre had persuaded the cook to part with. Despite the drizzle and gray clouds, there was an air of contentment around this small place.

"Sayre," Freeman whispered as he approached the stall.

Sayre looked up and continued her work.

"The captain's sent some men to get Warrior. They're having breakfast now."

She stopped, the rake held in midair and looked at Freeman. "I know. I'll have him ready when they finish eating."

Her face was frozen, and only one tear edged its way from her eye and down her cheek to drop and disappear into the ground below. She leaned the rake against the side of the stall, walked out of the stable, and took two brushes from the rack beside Warrior's stall. She began brushing him, back to front, easing the bristles around his wounds.

"I'll be out near the ravine. We've got some fences to fix today," Freeman said. "Gracie's in the corral with the black mare. I figured that horse needed the company more than any of the others."

His words came to a halt as he thought how foolish he sounded. But what do you say to someone whose heart is breaking all over again?

"Come on, Lady," he called. "We've got serious work to do, old girl, and I'm gonna need your help. Sayre, we'll be back this afternoon."

"Warrior," Sayre whispered, her hands moving over his body. "You've made these last two weeks more wonderful than I'd have thought possible. I was afraid I'd never see you again, and here you are. Now, here's what you and I have to do. You are going back to fight, so you have to be brave and, most importantly, you have to stay alive. I'll have to think of a way to find you wherever you are in this terrible war."

She stopped, went to the shelf, and took out a comb. Coming back, she held Warrior's head in her hands. He lowered his head and tucked it into her chest as she combed his forelock.

"You know if I could ride you out of here and back to the farm, I would, but I know just how far we'd get with our troops and Union troops everywhere and both looking for horses, especially one like you. There's nowhere for us to run. But I'm here, I'm close, and Freeman and I won't give up."

She brought his face up to hers, kissed the spot between his eyes, and began combing his mane. Then she moved to his tail, carefully grooming each hair. She picked each of his hooves, and then went to get the salve, which she carefully rubbed onto each wound one last time. When she had finished, she put a halter and lead rope on him and led him to the corral. Inside she mounted him and slowly paced him around the circle.

"You are lucky, Warrior," she cooed. "We are lucky. We're alive." She leaned down and rode this final time around with her head resting on his large, strong neck, savoring the scent of his mane.

When she had finished, she dismounted and walked Warrior to the stable, dropped his lead rope on the ground, and sat down next to him. It wasn't long before the men emerged from the hospital tent. They saw Sayre and the large chestnut horse and came to them.

"Looks good. Ready for the trip," the orderly said as he looked over the shining animal that stood quietly over Sayre. "Changed a lot since the last time I saw him."

"Yes, sir," Sayre replied. "I haven't trotted him much, haven't cantered or galloped him at all, but if he takes it easy for awhile, he'll be able to carry your captain wherever he wants to go."

"I'll tell the captain what you said. Thank you for all you've done for his horse."

Sayre's heart tightened at the words "his horse," for Warrior was nobody's horse but hers. However, her face did not betray her.

Sayre stood and handed Warrior's rope to the orderly and did not move as the man led her horse away. Only once did Warrior pull against the rope to turn and look at her. Just like that fateful day at the cave-stall, Sayre was powerless to stop him from being taken. She stood like a statue, mute and numb. When the figures on horseback had disappeared down the road, she finally turned, took the rake in her hands, and began mucking Warrior's stall. She sniffed the air, and was glad his scent lingered there.

CHAPTER 23

The next day, Mrs. Hill announced that the support camp would be moving out in two days. This ignited a frantic bustle of preparation in both the hospital and the stable.

Sherman's army was now advancing fast toward the North Carolina border. The general had been true to his pledge to "make Georgia howl" and had gone on to destroy everything in his path in South Carolina. Now North Carolina hunkered down, hoping it would be largely spared since it was a pathway to Virginia and, perhaps, an end to the war.

Freeman and Sayre began packing up once again, putting the huge trunks of stable supplies into the larger wagons and tying the sickest of their four-legged charges behind the smaller wagons. Sayre moved through the now mundane tasks, thinking only of Warrior.

"Sayre," Freeman finally ventured, "why don't you take it a bit easy today? I'll handle this. You were up all night, sitting by Warrior's stall reading your daddy's book by candlelight. Ain't good to go without sleep. This trip is gonna be hard, especially with the rain."

"I'm fine, Freeman. I couldn't sleep anyway, and, honestly, I feel okay. I can handle my part of the move. Mrs. Hill wouldn't take kindly to the stable boy moping around. She likes to see us busy."

Within two days, the wagons were loaded and on their way from South Carolina into North Carolina, taking on more injured horses and men as they went. As horses recovered, they were put into the herds at the end of the supply caravan until they were needed, thus making room for the newly wounded horses.

During the journey, Freeman and Sayre had stopped in horror at a field where a thousand horses, considered useless by Union commanders, had been herded into pens and shot as they whirled about in terror. This time, the search for survivors yielded only disappointment. Hundreds of the bloodied bodies floated in the Cape Fear River.

Tensions were high with rumors that Confederate cavalry under General Hamilton were skirmishing with Kilpatrick's troops almost everyday. General Joe Johnston had been called in to face Sherman somewhere along the road to Raleigh. Five days out, word came that there was a battle ahead, the last gasp of the dying Confederacy; the hospital and stables were again erected.

This time, the army combined two traveling regimental hospitals into a brigade hospital, which they housed in a large church. Nearby, the enormous barn of what had, until recently, been a prosperous farm became Freeman's new domain. He and Sayre wasted no time in making the place ready for a new surge of wounded animals.

Sally and the children kept busy rolling bandages and helping with the heaps of blood-soaked laundry. The days were bleak, chilly and wet, so getting wagons, people and herds of livestock here had not been easy. Everyone was tired and on edge, with no relief in sight from this endless, anxious work. The army had been on the march nearly four months.

Following a battle on March 21, 1865, the corral, stables, and hospital tents were filled almost to capacity. The fighting had been fierce and losses high for both Confederate and Union troops. The doctors and Mrs. Hill's nurses existed on only a few hours' sleep. The smell of the chloroform used in countless amputations reminded everyone at the camp of the sacrifices made in this war. Sayre and Freeman tended the wounded or jaded horses during the day, hardly glimpsing Parsy, Sally, or the children. Everyone was exhausted.

One evening, as Sayre made her last rounds and changed the dressing on the particularly bad wound on a thoroughbred mare, Freeman approached her. "Sayre," he said in a low voice, "Lt. Daniel is here. He's the young man who was posted at the farm when the army came by. Remember his horse Trace? Well, the lieutenant's been wounded pretty bad. One of the doctors had to amputate his leg today. I went to see him, and I was thinkin' you might stop in to check on him too. Maybe read to him?"

Sayre stared at Freeman trying to take in his words. She had successfully avoided contact with the Union soldiers unless they came to the stable, and then she'd only nodded and kept to her work. Tending their horses so that they could go on fighting against her people was one thing. But tending to the soldiers? They belonged to a world she wanted no part of. Suddenly, an anger that she did not recognize began to spill out.

She felt it pour forth from deep inside as she hissed, "I will not do anything more for this horrible army, for these Bluecoats who've destroyed my family, burned my home and stolen my horse! Look at us, working ourselves to the bone each day for the animals, their animals. I wouldn't care if every last soldier in Sherman's army was blown off the face of the earth and that includes Lt. Daniel. When he came through my farm, I had Warrior and my home. All that's changed now."

With that she ran from the stable, climbed to the top of the corral fence, and sat glaring into the darkness. She longed to see her father, to have her mother there beside her, and to once again ride through the woods on Warrior. The war had taken all these good things. She had tried to be brave and where had it gotten her? In her despair, she laughed at the answer: it had gotten her here, sitting on a fence, crying in North Carolina! And now Freeman was asking her to be kind to these invaders. Well, her answer was no and would remain no. No more! Just no more! She gripped the fence rails. Her chest heaved.

A soft, strong voice behind her said, "We've all known loss, Sayre. The last time I saw my wife she was bein' sold to a plantation in Mississippi. And the last time I saw my son, he was chained in a line of little boys sittin' by the side of the road. They were all crying while the slave traders yelled at them. Jeb was six years old. And there wasn't nothin' I could do but watch him go."

CHAPTER 24

*T*he next day, after the horses were fed and watered, ointments put on their wounds, some brushed and all talked to, Sayre left the stable area and made her way to the hospital. Since she rarely had a reason to enter Mrs. Hill's domain, the girl hesitated before opening the door and stepping inside.

After considering her limited options, Sayre had decided that a sturdy roll of bandages might bind her breasts tightly enough to achieve the flat chest required by her disguise. Although it had become harder, she was still passing for a boy. Clothes she'd stolen from the army successfully hid her figure. Her hands were so red and calloused from her work that they certainly did not look like a girl's hands. Her scissors ensured that her thick auburn curls stopped just below her ears in the style worn by most of the young men around her.

Sayre entered the hospital and moved between the rows of wounded soldiers to the trunks where the supplies were kept. Some of the wounded were on cots, others on bedrolls. It seemed that every inch of the church held a person. Her South was fighting hard, she thought.

Keeping her eyes straight ahead, she had almost reached the trunks when she heard a stifled sob coming from a cot to her right. She turned and saw Lt. Daniel lying there. The muffled sound was coming from him. Without thinking, Sayre found herself walking to the side of his bed. She was overwhelmed by the pallor of his skin and the tears falling from his eyes.

"Lt. Daniel," she said softly as the image of him and his black horse riding past her farmhouse flickered in her mind. "Lt. Daniel, it's me, Sayre Howard. I know you don't remember me, but you were kind to Freeman and me in Georgia. You kept the bummers from taking everything. You left us some food, and now we're tending the horses here."

The young man turned his face to her ,and his sobbing slowed. "My horse is dead. Trace is dead. They killed him. He was standing over me after I got shot. The Rebs shouldn't have killed him. He was just waiting for me to get up." And his tears began to flow again.

Sayre closed her eyes at this reminder that senseless cruelty flourished on both sides of this conflict. "I'm so sorry," she said. "I'm so sorry. Is there anything I can do?"

The lieutenant looked away. He had not mentioned the loss of his leg, only his beloved animal who had died so valiantly, so needlessly.

"I can read and I can write," Sayre volunteered. "May I write a letter to your family? Or read to you? Or," she paused, "I can just go away and not bother you. But I will tell you that I lost a horse once, one that I loved more than anything, and it hurt, it hurt a lot."

The young man turned his head to her. "What color was he?"

"He was ("is," she thought) a chestnut with a flaxen mane and tail that gleam like gold when the sun hits them. He was 15.2 hands, and a beauty. My papa and I raised him from a colt, and he would have stood over me to protect me if he knew I was in danger just like Trace did. I'm sure of that."

"Daddy and I raised Trace from a colt—only three years old when we bought him from a neighbor on the next farm.

He was eight when he died. I brought him with me because I didn't want to ride any horse but him, and now he's gone." A shudder reverberated through his body. "I should have left him at home."

"Well, my offer still stands," Sayre said. "I'm good at writing if you'd like. And maybe we could talk horses too. I'd like that. I could come back tonight after I finish working at the stable. That is, if you'd like me to."

"Well, I'll be here." He almost smiled at his feeble joke.

Sayre left the young soldier and got her bandages. When she walked back by Lt. Daniel's cot, his eyes were closed and he seemed to be resting more peacefully.

Outside, she made her way to Mrs. Hill's tent to find the indefatigable woman sitting at her desk, immaculately clad in a dark gray dress with her signature starched white cap and apron. Her brown hair was held neatly at the nape of her neck in a bun. She looked up from the pile of papers she was sorting, and did not speak.

"Mrs. Hill, excuse me" Sayre began. "I have just seen one of your soldiers in the hospital, Lt. Daniel. He was kind to us when the Federals came by our farm. I was wondering…" She slowed and took a breath before starting again. "I was wondering, first, if you could tell me how badly he's hurt, and second, would it be all right if I wrote a letter to his family for him, or read to him? I could come here after I finish my work at the stable."

"Sayre, I think that's a fine idea. You should know that Lt. Daniel is gravely wounded. He is only twenty two, another tragedy of this war that the South should never have begun. So, yes, you may tend to Lt. Daniel. Do you want to begin this evening after your work is completed at the stable?"

"Yes. Thank you, Mrs. Hill," Sayre said, then added hesitantly, "I'm afraid I have no pen and paper here."

"I'll leave some on the table by the entrance to the hospital. And, Sayre,"-the stern voice softened slightly—, "thank you."

When Sayre reached the stable, she looked for Freeman. He was in the corral working with several horses who were slowly winding their way back to health. As usual, Gracie and Lady were nearby.

"Freeman," Sayre said. "I just saw Lt. Daniel. His horse is dead. I'm going back this evening and read *Hamlet* to him since it's the story of a brave young man. I just wanted to let you know."

With that, she turned and walked toward the stalls. "Gracie," she called over her shoulder, "Come with me. I'm going to put one of the horses in the round pen and I need you to stay with him."

Gracie rose and followed Sayre as Freeman smiled. "Yep," he said softly to Lady, "the Howards taught her well."

When all of the stalls were cleaned, buckets washed and the horses bedded down for the night with fresh hay and water, Sayre decided to wash her hair and bathe in the creek, and put on her other set of clothes. She took Lady with her as a precaution against discovery and the other dangers of war. Even though the hospital camp was far behind the lines, Sayre knew enough to be cautious. Since it was only the beginning of spring, the weather was chilly and the creek water was cold, but she hardly noticed for her thoughts were only on Lt. Daniel and Trace.

When Sayre finished her hurried bath, she and Lady walked back to the stable where she picked up her precious, well-worn book, then headed for the hospital. Inside, she collected the paper, pen, inkwell, and oil lamp Mrs. Hill had left, and tiptoed to the cot where Lt. Daniel lay. Someone— presumably, Mrs. Hill—had thoughtfully placed a chair and small table near his bed. Sayre felt honored.

She sat down and softly spoke. "I'm here, Lt. Daniel. It's Sayre," she said as she placed the lamp on the table. "Would you like me to be your scribe or to read to you?"

She spoke hesitantly, looking down at his drawn face. He moved a bit and looked up at her. "Write a letter to my mama, if you don't mind," he said.

Sayre nodded and carefully placed the paper on the table so she could write more legibly, though there was only a little space available between the lamp and the edge of the table.

"Dear Mama," the lieutenant began. "Trace is dead. He died in the battle at Bentonville, but we won the battle and sent those Johnny Rebs running. I was hurt too, but am all right. I just want you to know I'm thinking of you, and I miss you, Papa, and Clarissa every day. It's rainy in North Carolina, but we're doing our best to stay dry. I love you. Say a prayer for me and Trace. Your loving son."

When Sayre finished the letter, she said, "I'll ask Mrs. Hill to send it out tomorrow."

"Would you help me sit up, Sayre?" Lt. Daniel asked. "And then, if that book you brought is for me, I'd appreciate it if you'd start a story."

"Certainly," she said.

A nurse hurried over to help lift him and prop the ragged pillow behind his back as Sayre opened the book and began.

Suddenly, the entire room became very quiet as her small voice hovered over the cots. "The scene is Elsinore on the platform before the castle. Enter to him Bernardo."

CHAPTER 25

"*S*ayre, Sayre, wake up." Freeman's excited voice startled her from a deep sleep in the stable where she still spent each night. "It's Trace. He's here. He's not dead!"

Sayre, still not yet awake, could not comprehend what he was saying. "Who?"

"Trace, the lieutenant's horse! He was just brought in with a group of sixteen horses. I thought I recognized him, and sure enough when I asked the handlers whose horse it was, they said he belonged to Lt. Daniel. He's wounded badly, but nothing worse than what we've seen already. It'd be good if you'd tell the lieutenant. I've got some men washing Trace down; then we'll figure out what we need to do next."

Sayre was now wide awake. She threw on her boots, pushed her hat over her curls, and ran to the hospital. There she saw the doctor and a nurse standing by Lt. Daniel's cot. She tentatively drew near. After a moment more of hushed conversation, they turned to look at her.

"I'm sorry to bother you this early, " she said. "but, the lieutenant thinks his horse is dead. He was very upset yesterday. It's all he could think about, really, but his horse has just been brought in, badly wounded but alive. I wanted Lt. Daniel to know."

The doctor responded while the nurse wiped sweat from the lieutenant's gaunt face. "Thank you. We'll tell him. He's taken a turn for the worse, but if he regains consciousness, we'll let him know. He's been calling out for 'Trace.' Is that the horse's name?"

"Yes, sir," Sayre said quietly. "It would mean so much to him to know Trace is alive. I'll be back at the stable if I can help."

As she reached the hospital's door, she whispered, "Please let him live to ride Trace again. He's a kind man, even if he is a Yankee."

Returning to the stable, Sayre ran to the stall where Freeman and another black man were laboring over Trace. The once-mighty animal had lost a lot of weight since Sayre had seen him only four months earlier, and there was a huge hole in his neck where a bullet had passed through. Sayre took a sponge and a rag and began rubbing him down, gently talking to him as she worked. The horse's eyes were flat and dull, but she had seen this look before. She knew she and Freeman had a chance of convincing the animal to hold on.

"Won't eat." Freeman said. "That's a problem. Got any molasses handy? We can tempt him with that. Throw a little on the corn feed."

"There's a bit left," Sayre said going to the shelf where the supplies were kept. "I've asked for some more, but it hasn't come yet."

She got some corn from the bin, then poured some molasses onto it, and carried it back to the stall. She held a handful of the mixture directly under the horse's mouth. He sniffed it, stuck out his tongue, tasted it tentatively, but then stood quietly, not eating any more.

Sayre spoke to him in a hushed tone. "You have been through so much, but you know what? Lt. Daniel is nearby. Your Lt. Daniel. He's alive and he wants to see you. You're all he thinks about. He thought you were dead, but you can't die now. You have to be strong for him. If you'll eat, that'll help. I'm going to put this in the feedbag, and when you feel like it, just taste it."

The stricken animal moved his head to look at her, then dropped it again.

Sayre walked to the feedbag and added the corn. Trace watched her every move, but stood silently, his ears barely flickering.

"Freeman, I'll take over your jobs today so you can focus all your attention on Trace," she said. "You have your hands full with him and the other new ones. When I'm finished I'll help you."

"That'll do," Freeman said as he carefully massaged the area around the horse's wound. "We're gonna work with him real good and see if we can't get some sparkle back into him."

The day was busy, busier than Sayre could imagine. At one point, Mrs. Hill came storming into the stable, a half-chewed black stocking in her hand. "Freeman," she yelled.

Freeman appeared from the corral, a dripping wet sponge in his hand. Sayre peeked out from a stall, but said nothing.

"Your goat! Where is she?"

"She was here a few minutes ago." His gaze took in the ruined stocking and the angry woman. "Gracie should be in the paddock. I was just about to put her in the stall with Trace. She does a powerful lot of good for horses too skittish to stay with other horses."

Mrs. Hill's eyes roamed the area, moving beyond Freeman to search for the goat.

Freeman's next strategy was distraction. "Here's some good news: we've got twenty two horses ready to return to duty. All mended and ready to ride. Parsy and his crew are rounding them up."

Mrs. Hill sighed. "I'm glad to hear your work is going well," she said, a note of irony in her voice, "but my stockings are not faring as well as your horses. That goat entered my tent, grabbed two stockings from where they were drying, and raced off with them. I found this one," she continued, holding up the shredded garment, "by the woodpile. If I see that animal anywhere near my quarters again, she will be dinner."

Freeman's face showed no emotion. "I'll find her, Mrs. Hill, and I'll find the other stocking. Sayre and I'll keep a special eye on Gracie from now on. Right, Sayre?"

The girl nodded vigorously, teetering between laughter and anxiety.

Hoping the encounter was reaching its conclusion, Freeman offered, "Please accept our apologies. First time Gracie's done anything like this."

"And, I can assure you, the last," Mrs. Hill muttered as she turned and strode resolutely back to the hospital.

Once Mrs. Hill was at a safe distance, Sayre grinned. "I'll go find the little demon, and I'll look for the stocking. C'mon, Lady, there's a thief in the camp and we have to find her right away."

When Sayre located the culprit, Gracie was in the paddock with the remnants of a second black stocking at her feet. She looked up, seeming quite pleased with herself as Sayre approached and picked up the ripped garment.

"Well, Gracie," she scolded, "you're in a lot of trouble. Now I have to take this thing back to Mrs. Hill and apologize. One more trick like this and you're done for. Remember, you're a walking main course, and food is mighty scarce."

Back at the stable, Sayre put Gracie into Trace's stall, then continued her work. It was late in the evening when she finished. The sun had already set and there was barely time to wash her hands and face. She went to her makeshift bed and slid the book of Shakespeare out from under it, ran to the hospital, and sat down next to Lt. Daniel. He was breathing softly and his eyes were open. He turned to Sayre as she approached.

"Is it true? Trace is here?" he asked.

"Oh, it's true all right. Freeman, Parsy, and some others spent a good part of the day working on him. I was there too. It's a bad wound, but I just know he'll make it. I told him you were here. That should help."

The young officer smiled.

"Would you like for me to finish *Hamlet* tonight? Then I can begin *Richard III*. There's a line in there I think you'll like, but I didn't tell you about it before, back before we knew Trace was alive. You see, King Richard has lost a battle and he's about to be killed or captured. He's on the battlefield, hoping to get away. He says, 'My horse! My horse! My kingdom for a horse!'"

Lt. Daniel smiled again, and whispered, "I'd like to hear that story." Then he paused, looked away. "Do you think they'll let me see Trace tomorrow?"

"I bet Mrs. Hill could arrange it." Sayre dropped her voice conspiratorially. "Everyone's afraid of her, they say even General Sherman. If she says you can see Trace, it will happen for sure."

With that Sayre opened the book and began reading. The miracle of Trace's arrival had so buoyed Sayre's spirit that she didn't feel at all sleepy. She read for what seemed like hours, once again moved by Hamlet's dilemma.

Somewhere near the end of the play, she heard the lieutenant sigh, and in a voice barely audible, he said, "Trace."

Sayre turned to look at him. His face was tranquil. She continued reading. She knew it was very late, for Mrs. Hill passed by making her final rounds before retiring for the evening.

Suddenly, Sayre was startled to see Freeman returning with Mrs. Hill. The two approached her.

Freeman spoke, "Sayre. Lt. Daniel's dead, Sayre."

"I know," she said.

Gently, she shut the book, leaned toward Lt. Daniel, and whispered. "At the very end, Horatio, who has always been such a good friend to Hamlet, whispers to him as Hamlet is dying, 'Good night, sweet prince, and flights of angels sing thee to thy rest.'"

CHAPTER 26

It was early morning when Sayre left the hospital. She carried a blanket to Trace's stall, sat down outside, and called for Lady to join her. The air felt cold, but refreshing. Sayre was wide awake, a hollow feeling in her stomach. She rested her hand on Lady's back and sighed.

"Warrior," she whispered to the still, dark air, "I've made a decision. There are a lot of letters to write and stories to read until this war ends. The color of uniforms doesn't really matter, I guess. I'll do what I can do. I bet Papa would agree. And I think Freeman's right that refusing to help these soldiers doesn't make anything better. Besides, if you need help, I'd want someone to help you. And if Papa needs help, I'd want someone to help him. I guess every living creature in this war needs help of some kind."

True to her word, that evening, Sayre again gathered her book and writing materials, and walked to the hospital. She found Mrs. Hill at her desk as usual.

"Come in, Sayre," the older woman said as she looked up.

"I've come to volunteer in the evenings," Sayre said.

"That will be fine," Mrs. Hill said. "I'm sure the soldiers will appreciate that. I'll let the doctors and nurses know you'll be here. You'll need to leave by eleven o'clock when I make the last rounds. I have an extra lamp you can take with you."

"Thank you, Mrs. Hill."

"And, Sayre," Mrs. Hill continued as Sayre started to leave, "this war will end soon and then we'll have to get along together, North and South."

Sayre nodded, found no words to speak, and left in silence.

When she entered the hospital, she summoned all of her courage and spoke to the men around her. "I would like to read to you or to write letters home for you. My name is Sayre Howard."

"I'd like that, son," an older man said. A huge, blood-stained bandage covered the right side of his head. "Come over here and sit. My wife'll be glad to know I'm alive."

With that invitation, Sayre took a deep breath, walked to the cot, positioned her pen and paper, and began as the soldier dictated, "Dear Edna."

From then on, the days and nights at the camp fell into a pattern: Sayre tirelessly tended to wounded animals during the day and wrote letters for wounded soldiers during the evening. She finished the nights by reading aloud to the men. She hoped the words from the three hundred-year- old stories would lull the patients to sleep or at least take their minds off their pain.

Gradually, Sayre started to talk with the soldiers. She learned about their lives from the letters the men dictated, and soon they were sharing stories of home and of family, of loss and of hope. When one soldier mentioned how he'd made a point of pressing leaves between the pages of the Bible he carried with him, Sayre told him about her collection of feathers and brought one to him the next day.

One evening when she walked into the hospital, she found a magnificently brilliant cardinal feather in the middle of the floor. She gasped with happy surprise as she stooped to pick it up. When she rose to show the men, she realized that every single one of them was looking away.

Sayre smiled, realizing what had happened. "Thank you," she said to the soldiers around her, and she placed the feather in her book.

In the wake of that small act of kindness, Sayre found herself wanting to tune her papa's fiddle and play it softly when she was alone. Tunes like "Amazing Grace," "Aura Lee," and "Hard Times Come Again No More" spilled from the old instrument. Trace, Magic, Gracie and Lady were her audience. Still, Sayre couldn't bring herself to play her papa's livelier songs, the tunes that made every foot in the room tap. Parts of her ached too deeply to brush away the ghosts of her losses, ghosts conjured by the music.

At night, Sayre still slept outside Trace's stall. She and Freeman worked tirelessly to make sure his recovery was complete. Their great triumph was Magic, who was now in a small pasture near the stable. Several times during the week, Sayre saddled and rode him around the pasture, never venturing far, but overjoyed to again be a rider with a horse. Magic was a smooth ride: his walk was full of vigor, his trot was fluid, and his canter was soft and collected. Clearly, someone had trained him well.

One day melded into the next, until finally the camp was once more on the move toward Raleigh. The promise of spring was in the air, its sweet, pungent smell filling the air around them like the birdsongs that grew ever livelier with mating and nesting calls.

Trace was better, less lethargic, but certainly not the prancing stallion Sayre remembered from a long-ago day in Georgia. There were still wounded animals coming in, usually from small skirmishes with the Confederates, but there was now money from Washington for new uniforms, equipment and rations, which streamed into the Union camp and lifted morale. A troop of well-dressed black troops even joined the cavalcade.

On a particularly balmy spring evening, as Sayre launched into an animated reading of *The Taming of the Shrew*, a new favorite among the men, she was interrupted by loud shouts. Marking her place in the book, she ran to the church's door and saw a messenger riding into camp. He whirled his horse around, yelling all the while and waving his hat frantically in the air. He was immediately surrounded by soldiers from throughout the camp.

"Lee has surrendered to Grant at Appomattox, Virginia! Two days ago. Remember the date, boys: April 9, 1865. The war's over!"

The hospital erupted in whoops of excitement. Mrs. Hill came racing from her tent and, upon hearing the news, astonished everyone by joining in the revelry.

"We've won," she shouted. "Boys, you'll be going home just like Mr. Lincoln said. Now I want you to promise me you'll get well and be ready to celebrate, you hear me?"

She paused when she saw Sayre standing quietly, her hands clutching her papa's book.

"Sayre, I'd like to see you in my office now."

"Yes, ma'am," Sayre replied and followed the woman while the camp continued its joyful uproar.

Sayre walked into the tent that served as Mrs. Hill's bedroom and office. The lamp on the small desk bathed the room in a comforting light.

"Sayre," Mrs. Hill began, seating herself in the chair, "I know the news of this surrender must be difficult for you. While I am overjoyed to have this ghastly war over, I am sorry that this conclusion grieves you. I so admire what you and Freeman have done for the animals and for the men even though they, we, are not on your side. You've worked very hard." The woman hesitated, then seemed to come to her primary point, "Why are you and Freeman really here? I know there's some story involved. Will you tell me? Of course, you don't have to answer if you don't want to."

Sayre stood very still. She was quite taken aback by the interest shown by this stalwart woman whom she admired.

As she spoke, her voice quavered. "Some Union bummers stole my horse, and most of our food, and burned my house. I couldn't let them just take my horse, so we set out to find Warrior, that's his name, and bring him back home to be there when my papa comes back." And her voice dropped. "If he does come back."

After a moment of studying the floor, Sayre continued. "Freeman and I started out alone. Then, after Ebenezer Creek, Freeman thought we'd be safer with you, with the Union Army. Warrior was actually here with us for a couple of weeks. He was badly wounded, but we were able to make him well. Then we sent him off to the officer who now owns him. So I've lost him twice."

Suddenly overcome by emotion, Sayre abruptly turned to leave. But then paused and continued, "Thank you for asking, for caring. I've learned a lot here, and people have been kind. War is very confusing. It hurts so many. I know we still have a lot of work to do here with the horses. Then, when the right time comes, Freeman and I will head home. And somehow, we'll have Warrior with us."

Mrs. Hill sat very still, then said, "We've all learned a lot, Sayre. This war has been a stern teacher."

Sayre nodded and, deep in thought, walked back to the stable. She turned toward Trace's stall to check on him once more before going to bed. The horse knew her footsteps and whinnied a greeting. She began to rub behind his ears, a gesture she knew he liked.

" Congratulations, Trace, your side won. The war's over and..." She spoke her remaining words very carefully and softly, each word hanging in her throat. "My South has been defeated."

Sayre stood for a long time, caressing the horse's head, then lay down and dreamt of home.

CHAPTER 27

$\mathcal{T}$he troops guarding the rear of the Union Army were jubilant at the defeat of the South. They were heading for Richmond, Virginia, the capital of the Confederacy. They were going there as conquerors and heroes. Old Lee Johnson was to meet Sherman in that city to surrender, and word was spreading that the Confederate president, Jefferson Davis, had fled southward. There was to be a huge parade in Washington. New uniforms and rations were to be issued soon and back pay was also on its way for the many soldiers who had not seen a paycheck in months.

Sayre and Freeman, now with two horses, Trace and Magic, tied behind their wagon, rode with their hospital unit toward Washington. Lady sat alertly between them. Nearby, Parsy drove another wagon carrying his family. At his side, Sally held the two babies, Jonah and Moses, on her lap, and they cooed at Gracie, who rode in the back with the other children.

Sayre's thoughts were of her father and Warrior. Where were they now that the war had ended?

When the vast caravan stopped in the evenings, she continued to read to the wounded men and to write letters home, letters which now were filled with anticipation of reunions with their loved ones. With the war finally over, men could think again of building a barn, planting a field, or opening a business in town.

143

For their part, Freeman and Parsy argued over what would happen to the South. It had become a nightly ritual that each man enjoyed at the campfire.

"I'll rely on President Lincoln any day to let us go on our way, give us land to farm." Freeman asserted.

"You don't think he'll keep his army in the South?"

"From what I've heard, I don't think he will," Freeman replied.

"I think the North will punish 'em." Parsy countered.

"But didn't you hear about Grant at Appomattox? I heard it from a soldier in camp. Said every Confederate cavalryman was entitled to take his horse home with him. Said it was important because the soldiers wouldn't be able to plant spring crops without their horses. That tells me what's going on."

"Maybe. But how are the Southerners gonna look on us folks who used to be their slaves? I like the idea of free land to farm, but I'm nervous. I'm gonna move my family up north, near Washington. There's plenty of work up there. What you gonna do?"

"Reckon I'll ride home with Sayre, see if his pa makes it home too. Then I'll get to farming. We need to find his horse first, though. I told you that's what this has been about. If you hear anything about Warrior, you let me know. That horse was with some officer but we don't know which one, so it's like trying to find a needle in a haystack."

"Well, I'll keep my ears open for word of his father or his horse. Sayre is a mighty fine boy and my children have taken a liking to him. He's been teaching the older ones to read and now the younger ones wanna learn too. Beats all. I'm afraid he'll soon come after me with that big book of his."

The two men laughed.

"I expect we'll get to Washington in about a month. We've got a good bit of traveling to do to get there," Freeman said, "but at least we won't be getting many more wounded men or animals. That'll make life simpler. Got pretty complicated for a while. Never seen such suffering and I don't want to witness any more. We saw a lot of good and brave horses die. It wasn't their war, but they suffered just the same. Always do, I guess, as long as we rely on 'em."

"I'll not forget Ebenezer Creek, no matter how long I live," Parsy said. "Looking for those bodies and seeing my people stranded on the other side with nowhere to go between the Rebs and the water. Still dream of that night. Wake up sweating."

"That was a tough one, all right. It's been some trip. Never thought I'd do this, but it ain't been all bad. Horribly sad at times, but that's part of life too. Met some fine folk like you, Parsy."

They both fell silent.

Freeman finally rose and said, "Well, I'd better turn in. More traveling tomorrow. I'll go check on Sayre."

He was halfway to the hospital wagons and tent when the sound of galloping hooves made him stop. Lady began to bark loudly. It was very late for anyone to be out and Freeman was concerned.

One rider on a sweating black horse galloped past him, halted at Captain Bradford's tent, dismounted, and raced inside. The soldiers who rode with him remained mounted until the messenger emerged, remounted and, alone, rode back the way he had come. The other soldiers dismounted and men from the camp took charge of their horses.

An orderly ran from Captain Bradford's tent and Freeman called to him as he hurried past, "What's happened?"

Without pausing the young man blurted, "President Lincoln has been shot. He's dead. All hell's breaking loose. Gotta spread the word," and he raced off toward the hospital.

The newly arrived soldiers quickly began surrounding the camp, their rifles ready to stop any intruders, for no one knew how deep the plot to destabilize the government might be. As news of the catastrophe in Washington spread, mayhem reigned for several minutes. Then an eerie silence filled the camp.

Sayre ran from the hospital to the stable. "Is it true, Freeman? Lincoln's dead?"

"'Fraid so. "Don't look good. He was a fair man. He'd have looked after the South and the slaves. Now it's anybody's guess what'll happen."

"I'm going back to the hospital. Some of the men there are very worried, and I'll see if I can help calm them. Sally's there too. I guess we need to be ready for anything."

"You're right," Freeman replied. "Lady and I'll look in on all the horses one last time and then try to catch a little sleep." He put his hand on the dog's head, and she looked up at him. "Reckon I'll get out my rifle, Lady. Don't know who's wanderin' around here with all this mischief going on. Guess we'll all remember April 17, 1865, as one of the sadder days we've known. A great man died today. Wish he'd stayed around so we could thank him."

CHAPTER 28

*L*ittle was known but much was feared about the shadowy forces that might seek to destabilize the nation. As Union troops converged on Washington, other camps were thought to be at greater risk, so the camp's guards were reassigned, leaving only a thin sentry detail at Mrs. Hill's hospital and Freeman's stable. As Sayre watched the patrols ride away, she was not alone in feeling that her small herd of recuperating horses was now vulnerable. It was a very isolated Union camp that now held a gold mine of healthy horses.

That night, three mounted Confederate soldiers slipped noiselessly through the trees to the corral where the horses were kept. They were on a raiding mission because, even though the war was over and the peace treaty signed, Southerners were desperate to claim horses to help them return home and start a fresh life.

A small, wiry man dismounted and pulled two boards from the fence, setting them on the ground and creating an opening big enough to get the horses out. He remounted expertly. Nearby Lady growled, then barked. There was no time to lose. The second man moved his horse into the corral and maneuvered the animals toward the opening. Only one large bay horse refused to move as the other nine horses trotted away. The three men closed around and behind them, then raced off into the darkness.

Too late, Freeman's rifle blared a wake-up call to the Union soldiers who ran to their mounts and began saddling them. Freeman sprinted to where Magic was pacing back and forth, the only one left in the corral.

"Good boy, good boy," Freeman said to the horse as he put on the halter, threw the blanket and saddle on his back, and jumped on.

"Did you see which way they went?" a sergeant shouted to Freeman as three Union soldiers galloped up beside him.

"That way." Freeman pointed to the pasture and the woods that lay beyond.

"Then let's go," the soldier said, and motioned for the men to follow him. "But let's go slowly. There could be more Rebels out there waitin' to ambush us. Did you see how many came in?"

"I saw three, but could be more," Freeman answered.

By now they were entering the dark woods that surrounded the corral. They stopped their horses and were quiet, listening for the sound of hooves moving ahead of them.

Freeman and the sergeant pushed their mounts at a trot in the direction of the fleeing Confederates. Within minutes they were on the banks of a small river. The current in front of them was turbulent, but upstream the moonlight showed men swimming the small herd across to the other side.

"I guess these Johnnies know the place to ford. Come on, let's skirt the river through the trees and cross up there. I don't want to lose anyone, man or animal, in that water," the sergeant said. "When we get across, we'll see what comes next. I don't know if any part of the Confederate army is 'round here, so these men could be operating on their own."

Soon they reached the spot where the river, though still swift, could be safely forded, and the four Union soldiers and Freeman plunged into the water. The men slid from their saddles and held on tightly as the horses swam across and then staggered forward when their hooves hit solid ground on the far side.

Remounting, they took off at a fast gallop, hoping to overtake the raiding party as it wound its way down a road where burned-out farmhouses stood on each side. The silhouettes of the men and horses ahead told them they were on the right track.

The trap that fell on them was silent and complete. Behind them five mounted men bolted from a barn while three more cut off their escape from the front. All had guns pointed at the pursuers. There was nothing left to do but halt.

A large man in a ragged Confederate uniform spoke, "Now, fellows, just sit here for a while and let the boys get the horses away. No need for any quarrels between friends. Drop your guns on the ground. Slowly, now. Do as I say."

All five complied, cautious not to do anything that would cause these desperate men to shoot. The war was over. This was no time or place to die.

"Now," the leader commanded. "You four soldiers dismount slowly and start walking back. Thanks for adding four more horses to our catch tonight. We'll take the black man with us. Get moving. Run!

The four Union soldiers did as they were told, sprinting down the road. Soon they had veered back toward the river, vanishing into the darkness of the woods.

One Confederate dropped out of his saddle to collect the guns from the road. Freeman sat astride Magic, trying to plan his next move.

When the four Union soldiers had disappeared, the leader spoke to Freeman, "Come on with us. I'm sure there's a farm back home that could use an extra hand."

Freeman was silent and turned Magic into the center of the eight riders and squeezed him into a trot. They'd not proceeded more than a few minutes when the noise of approaching hoofbeats brought the party to a stop. The soldiers turned their mounts to the sound, their guns ready.

The leader barked, "Don't fire. It could be Sergeant Blake. He's been reconnoitering in the area and I don't know if he's returned yet."

The lone rider drew near. Astonished, Freeman saw that it was Sayre. She was on Trace, her hat pulled tight on her head and her face a study in determination.

Freeman spoke in a hushed, but strong voice. "Don't shoot! That's my master."

Sayre reined Trace in and boldly faced Freeman's captors. "You have my slave. My papa's been fighting for two years with Lee. Our farm or what's left of it is near Griswoldville, Georgia." Pointing to Freeman, she said, "I need this man back and I'd say thirteen horses is a fair trade for him, wouldn't you? I'm not armed. It wouldn't do any good anyway. Two more dead people won't matter, but if you kill him, you'll have to kill me too. We've been through a lot together."

The leader asked, "How old are you, son?"

"I'm fourteen," Sayre replied. "I'm old enough to have lost my mother, my father and everything else in the world that matters to me. That makes me a lot older than fourteen and I don't intend for Southerners to do me more harm than the Bluebellies have."

"Then what was the black man doing helping the Union chase after us if you're so Southern?" demanded another of the men.

"The only way we could survive on the road was to hook up with the Union Army. We originally started out trying to get to my relatives in Charleston," Sayre lied, "but that didn't work out. We were forced to work with the Union's wounded horses. All I'm asking is for you to let us go home, back to Georgia. I just hope your farm hasn't been burned like mine."

The leader looked around. His men still held their guns pointed at Freeman and Sayre. He looked at the determined face of the young man in front of him and thought of his own son. They had the horses. None of his men had been killed. The war was over.

He spoke to his men, "Let them go. We've got miles to cover. You two are free to go. Ride back to the camp and leave us to our work."

With that, the Confederates turned their horses and began to gallop away. Sayre glanced at Freeman and then touched her heels to Trace's sides, gently asking the horse to move forward at a walk. Freeman did the same with his horse. Then, without warning, the last Confederate soldier wheeled his mount around, raced a few steps toward Freeman and Sayre, and opened fire on the two. One bullet whistled past Sayre's head, another found its mark and Freeman slumped in his saddle before tumbling to the ground.

Magic froze when Sayre screamed and pulled Trace to a halt. She dismounted quickly and ran to where Freeman lay, his shoulder bleeding profusely. Sayre looked up the road only to see the Confederates racing away. Fighting back panic, she reached under her shirt and untied the bandages that bound her chest, and began to soak up the blood pouring from the wound.

Freeman stirred, and his eyes flickered open.

"It's all right," Sayre said. "I'm trying to stop the bleeding from your shoulder. The soldiers are gone. I just need to get you out of this road. There might be other troops in the area, Confederate or Union. It's not safe here. Please, Freeman. Can you help? There's a barn over there. Can you sit up?"

"I reckon I'll try," Freeman said as he struggled up, groaning with each movement.

When he was almost standing, his knees buckled. Sayre watched in horror as he fell back to the dirt, his blood staining the roadside.

She spoke with renewed urgency, "Try again, please," she urged and she reached around his uninjured side.

This time Freeman stood, staggered slightly, but stayed upright. Together, the two struggled toward the barn. Straining under her companion's weight, Sayre fixed her eyes on the small rickety structure, dismayed by how slowly they closed the distance. Finally, they reached the shelter and Freeman slumped onto the ground, his back against the old wooden boards.

Sayre ran back to lead Trace and Magic from the road. Once the two horses were secured in the barn, she sat down next to Freeman, her thoughts racing. Not only was he wounded, but she now understood how vulnerable they were in these volatile times. The end of the war and the murder of the president had created a vacuum, a no-man's land of lawlessness. She couldn't leave Freeman here alone. But he urgently needed medical care.

Hope flared at the thought that the Union soldiers who'd ridden out with Freeman might get fresh horses and come back this way in pursuit of the Confederates. But would they think to look here for a black man and a Southern boy? Would they care what had happened to them?

Fighting despair, Sayre moved to the door of the barn, looked around, but could make out nothing in the moonless night. She shuddered. There were no sounds except the rhythmic beats of the cicadas' songs and Freeman's labored breathing. Sayre was terrified. Freeman moaned slightly. She turned to check on his shoulder, then sat down heavily on the ground beside him, her knees tucked up to her chin.

Suddenly there was the sound of an animal running down the road. A deer? Something bigger? Whatever it was, it was traveling fast. Sayre rose and took a few tentative steps toward the road, aware that she had no gun and was essentially defenseless. She squinted into the darkness and was astonished to see a familiar form materialize. Lady stopped in the road and sniffed the air.

"Lady," Sayre called in a relieved whisper, "Come here, come here, girl!"

The dog trotted toward her.

"Good girl," Sayre said, a plan instantly forming in her mind. "You must stay to guard Freeman. I'll ride back to the camp. Stay."

The large dog looked up at the girl, then walked to where Freeman sat. She lay her head on his lap. Freeman's hand came up to pat her gently. He opened his eyes.

"Freeman, I'm going for help. You and Lady wait for me. Right here."

Sayre untied Trace, walked him from the barn, and mounted.

"Guess we don't have any important place to go at the moment," Freeman said, trying to ease the worry he saw on the girl's face. "We'll be right here." Then his face tightened into a grimace as a wave of pain ran over his body.

Not allowing herself to look back at the man who'd been her stalwart companion ever since her mother's death, Sayre grabbed Trace's reins more tightly. With a kick, the horse and rider raced away.

Sayre and Trace raced down the dark road, across the river, and through the woods. With relief that made her dizzy, she saw the camp ablaze with light from fires set around its perimeter. Clearly, everyone was on the alert since the soldiers had returned and related their experience with the Confederate raiding party.

Sayre yelled to the sentry, who raised his gun to challenge her entry. "It's me, Sayre, from the stable."

The guard stepped aside and Sayre hurried forward. Pulling Trace to a halt, she jumped from the saddle, shouting, "Parsy, Parsy! Come quickly! Freeman's been shot and I need help!"

Parsy appeared at a run with his wife close behind. "You've got it," he called, already heading for his horse. "Sally, get some hot water and bandages ready."

Within minutes, the two were riding back to the abandoned barn, and when there, Parsy leapt from his horse and went to Freeman's side.

"Well, look at you," he said, "You've gone and got yourself shot so you'd look good for the parade in Washington, is that it? Like you'd been fighting or something?"

Then, dropping any attempt at levity, he reached down and began carefully lifting Freeman to his feet.

"Sayre, move Magic over to that low piece of ground outside the barn. That way the stirrup won't be so high once I guide Freeman over there. Now, Freeman, give us a little help here. One foot up, that's it, and the other leg over. Now you're gonna have to hold on. Just balance for me.

Using all his strength, Freeman mounted the horse and sat as tall as his wound would allow.

With Freeman in the saddle, Parsy spoke to Sayre, "You ready to ride Trace?"

"No, you ride. I want to walk with Lady. She and I will keep an eye on Freeman."

Parsy mounted Trace, and Sayre handed him Magic's reins. Freeman clung to the saddle, his eyes still closed. Parsy moved the horses forward slowly as Sayre and Lady walked vigilantly alongside. No one spoke.

When they reached the river, the two horses paddled with their riders in their saddles. Sayre and Lady swam beside them. Regaining dry ground, Parsy carefully picked a path through the woods so that Freeman would be safe from low-hanging branches. Still, through his drenched shirt, blood seeped from Freeman's wound.

Their progress was agonizingly slow and Sayre breathed more easily when the camp was finally in sight. Her relief vanished when Parsy headed for the stable. "No, this way, we've got to get him to the hospital," she said.

Parsy looked at her strangely. "Sayre, they ain't gonna take a black man up there."

"But it's Freeman. And...and...I'll..."

Parsy shook his head, not unkindly, and moved steadily away from the hospital and toward the stable. After assisting Parsy as he pulled Freeman from the saddle, Sayre ran to find Mrs. Hill, sure that the woman could help them get the care that Freeman needed.

Mrs. Hill was still working, the lamp on her desk casting dark shadows on the wall of the tent that was her makeshift office.

Sayre burst in breathlessly, slinging drops of water from her still-drenched clothes. "Mrs. Hill, ma'am, Freeman's been shot. He needs a doctor right away. Please."

Mrs. Hill's face was awash with concern. "I'll get Dr. Young immediately," she said, rising from her desk. "Where is he?"

"Parsy took him to the stable, but I know he'd be better off in the hospital."

There was a brief pause before the woman replied, "Sayre, you go back and stay with him, make him comfortable. I'll get the doctor. I'm afraid we don't have a place for him"- Mrs. Hill cleared her throat- "in the hospital."

"The stable will be fine," Sayre replied and turned to leave.

"Sayre, wait." Mrs. Hill's voice carried a different note and Sayre turned back . Mrs. Hill looked confused. "Wait here. You…I see…well, let me get you a jacket. Your clothes are very wet."

Sayre, frightened by Freeman's condition and angered by his treatment, stared at the woman in utter consternation. This was no time to worry about soggy clothing, not when Freeman had been shot.

Then, suddenly, it was clear to her. Sayre glanced down and saw how the layers of wet shirts clung to her now-unbound breasts. She raised her head as Mrs. Hill re-entered the room carrying a brown jacket, which she handed to Sayre, saying only, "Go tend to Freeman. I'll fetch the doctor and some supplies."

Sayre awkwardly pulled the garment over her clammy shirts, murmuring, "Thank you, ma'am, for helping us, both of us."

Sayre ran back to the stable and knelt next to Freeman, who was stretched out on his cot, his eyes closed, his breath shallow, his face pale. Parsy, Sally, Lady, and Gracie stood nearby.

"Thank you, Parsy. The doctor's on his way." Sayre stared at Freeman's bandage, watching as the red stain conquered more and more of the white fabric.

CHAPTER 29

D r. Young's voice penetrated the tense stillness,
"Sally, bring the water. And help me with these
bandages."

"I've got the water right here, and the children and I just
finished scraping some lint."

"Excellent. That's precisely what we need to staunch this
bleeding. Parsy, here's my flask. It might help to give the
patient a swallow of whiskey."

As the last layer of hastily wrapped bandaging fell away
in the doctor's hands, Freeman's wound became visible. Dr.
Young peered at it, then checked the top of Freeman's chest,
which they now saw was pierced with an exit wound.

"That's lucky. Looks like it's a clean shot. Bullet went
straight through. What a mercy. Help me rinse it off, then
we'll pack it with lint and bandage him again."

Sayre watched the doctor work. The fluffy fibers of
Sally's lint were soon packed into the wound and bandaged
into place to stop any further bleeding. Although beads of
sweat appeared on his forehead, Freeman lay still and quiet
except for an occasional moan.

Dr. Young straightened up and gathered his instru-
ments. "We'll see how he fares for the rest of the night. I'll
check on him when I'm finished in the hospital, but let me
know immediately if there's a change for the worse. Good-
night to you."

Sally watched him walk back in the direction of the hospital, then placed her hand on Sayre's arm. "I need to go check on the children, but let us know if Freeman needs anythin'."

"Thank you," Sayre said. She moved quietly to one of the trunks that held some tack, opened the lid, and took out her box of feathers and her book of Shakespeare. Then she settled down on the soft dirt next to Freeman's cot, her treasures in her lap, her back against the stall door. She laid her hands atop the book and its presence comforted her. Magic's head, then Trace's head, appeared above her. Parcy had put them in two adjacent stalls after the night's adventure where they had played so prominent a role. Lady and Gracie sat nearby. They would all be right there when Freeman opened his eyes.

Sayre stared into space, stunned by the evening's events and wishing so much that Freeman could hear her thoughts. They had come so far, and a world without Freeman was too bleak to contemplate. He had honored her dream of finding Warrior and her determination to set something right in this topsy-turvy war-torn world. He had always been there for her.

"A world without Freeman," she spoke it aloud and felt small and alone, riding once more on events she couldn't control. She pulled Lady next to her. Gracie moved closer too and the three of them began their vigil.

When the sky began to glow with the first light of the sun, Freeman stirred and opened his eyes. "Sayre," he whispered.

She was immediately at his side. Lady and Gracie followed her.

"You're safe, Freeman. You're here in the barn. Dr. Young says the wound is clean. You just have to rest. Sally and I are fine nurses, and"- she pointed at the dog and the goat- "We have help from these two."

"Well, that's quite a team," Freeman answered, a weak smile lighting his face.

"My goal is to have you in good shape to see that parade in Washington and to help me find Warrior. I consider this just a minor setback."

Freeman smiled again and closed his eyes. "I'm a minor setback," he murmured and went back to sleep.

Sayre went to the well, drew a bucket of water and splashed some of the cool liquid on her face. She went to her small room, used fresh bandages to bind her breasts, layered on three fresh shirts, and cinched the rope that held the garment around her waist. Since she had lost a good bit of weight over the preceding six months, the pants fit even more loosely than when she'd first put them on in her Georgia farmhouse.

The attack on Freeman had freshly demonstrated that peril still surrounded them. She was simply unready to reveal to everyone that she was a girl. Her disguise had become a major part of her war-tinted reality, and she was surprised to realize that it might take some time for her to return to feminine ways.

Of course, with Freeman injured, nothing else was of much consequence. As her thoughts returned to her wounded companion, she realized that her hands were trembling. There was work to do and she cast about for some way to dispel the panic now invading her every thought.

Sayre closed her eyes and whispered, "Papa. Warrior," then willed the trembling to stop.

Taking a deep breath, she headed out to the barn. Sayre fed and cared for the more seriously wounded horses that the Confederates had left behind. Parsy brought three men to move Freeman and his cot to the corner of the barn near a vacant stall, where he could rest away from all the hubbub. In between chores, Sayre checked on her friend.

She was re-bandaging a horse's leg when a deep voice behind her called her name. She turned to see Quartermaster Bradford, head of the camp, standing there. "How is Freeman?" he asked.

"He's slept most of the day. Dr. Young has done all he can and says resting is the thing Freeman needs now. We just have to wait and see."

"The doctor's right, I'm sure. He's one of the best I've seen. I've come to tell you we'll be breaking camp tomorrow. We're heading into Virginia, the last leg of this journey to Washington. I'm sure you've heard the government is planning a huge parade there to honor the men who have served their country so valiantly through this long and arduous war. He turned to go, then continued. "This is the first time I've been back here to see your operation. Parsy has kept me informed on your day-to-day activities, and Mrs. Hill has told me of your kindness to our wounded men. Impressive. And the goat?"

Sayre smiled, "Gracie's with Freeman. She sticks close to him or the horses. That way she doesn't end up in a stew. She's quite clever."

Captain Bradford's face broke into a smile. "My wife is never going to believe the stories about Gracie and how she has survived the war, or Mrs. Hill's wrath. It's one of the few bright spots I can tell her. Remember, Sayre, we leave tomorrow, early. Do you think Freeman can travel or will we need to dismiss you two and make arrangements for others to look after the animals?"

"No, sir. We'll be ready. All of us." Sayre hoped she sounded more confident than she felt and she resolutely resumed her work.

The quartermaster nodded and left her to her duties.

When she was sure he was gone, Sayre spoke to the horses around her, "I'll just have to make sure Freeman is able to travel tomorrow. Freeman was right. Our survival depends on staying with you and your army." She paused, then added, "You're also our best chance to find Warrior."

The next morning, just past sunrise, the camp was alive with activity. Wounded men were placed in wagons or ambulances, the trunks of tack and supplies from the stable and the hospital were loaded onto other conveyances with the injured horses tied behind.

Parsy and Sally's family and a few hands in the stable had helped Sayre get ready for the move, though it had meant another sleepless night. Freeman was able to ride propped up in the back of the wagon, a quilt over him to keep the chill off which lingered in the May air, Sayre drove with Lady on the seat beside her while Gracie sat in the back by Freeman's side.

The army moved quickly through southern Virginia encountering slaves still working in the fields. Though Lincoln's Emancipation Proclamation had freed them two years earlier and a war had since been fought and won, many had not been told the news.

Sayre began to see more ragged Confederate soldiers straggling past the wagon train, heading south. The Union soldiers around her offered these refugees food, strong coffee or a plug of tobacco, then sat around the campfires at night and talked with them as if they were old friends. Each side was alive with stories of the war, and all agreed they were tired of the fighting and just wanted to go home. The adventure was over, and they were glad they had survived.

Sayre studied each man and each horse she saw, hoping her father or Warrior would appear. Neither materialized, and soon she was just hoping for a miracle.

It was late in the evening and Sayre had just finished reading to the wounded men and writing a few letters for them. She was walking from the church that was serving as the hospital back to the shed where the horses were kept. Since the night was chilly, she wore the jacket Mrs. Hill had given her and had her hat pulled snugly over her hair. She was thinking about getting back to see Freeman, who was now able to sit up for short periods of time. She was tired, though the evening of reading to the soldiers had gone well and she had enjoyed chatting with them.

She stopped suddenly when she recognized a voice close to her, and then a chill raced through her body. Quickly and silently she stepped behind a huge oak tree, every pore in her body focused on the conversation.

"So, Joe," a man said, "what ya gonna do after the war? You've sure made a name for yousef. Almost as well known as ole Bill Sherman! Some say you supplied the Union Army singlehandedly with what you stole."

Joe laughed. "Did my part fer sure. The officers shore liked the horses I rounded up fer 'em. Handsome animals. If the army don't need me anymore, I'll go home to Tennessee, but first I'm gonna talk to Captain Henry to see what he can do fer me. He owes me big 'cause of that horse I stole fer 'im , one of the best Saddlebreds I came across in Georgia."

"That was one magnificent animal," the other man replied. "Didn't think he would make it after he was wounded so bad at Barnwell, but he and the cap came back as good as new. I know the cap's alive. Know anything about the horse?"

"Nope," Joe replied. "Haven't heard a word. I know the cavalry is still fighting the Rebs, and the captain's part of that. Seems some don't know to just give up and call it quits. Do know both sides lost a lot of animals. Back in the early days of the war, a horse would only last about six months. Don't know the odds now."

"Who'll you be ridin' with in the parade?" the other man asked.

"Probably with Kilpatrick's cavalry. Feel more at home with them. Made some pretty good friends there. I gotta get my gear cleaned up, though. Sure want Sherman to be proud when we ride by. I'm headin back now. Just came to see a friend here at the hospital. He won't be in the parade. Didn't make it. A good fella and a good bummer. Too bad. So close to the end."

"See ya, Joe. I'll look ya up in Washington."

"Right," Joe responded.

Sayre waited until she couldn't hear any sounds near her, then carefully peered around the huge trunk of the tree. She stood motionless for a few minutes. Then she began to walk and finally to run.

"Freeman," she called as she neared his cot. He turned his head to look at her as she knelt down beside him. "We have to find a way to go to the parade in Washington. The man who stole Warrior was here in camp, and I heard him talking about Captain Henry and his horse. I don't know for sure if he was talking about Warrior, or if my horse is alive, but if it is Warrior and he is alive, he'll be in the parade with the captain riding as part of Kilpatrick's cavalry."

Freeman's face lit up. "Well then, we still have a chance of findin' 'im. We're still in the game." And he struggled to sit up.

"Do you think they'll let us near Pennsylvania Avenue? After Lincoln's assassination, Southerners may not be welcome."

"Well, they still want us tending their horses. Let's talk with Parsy."

Sayre added, "And I'll check with Mrs. Hill. If we see Warrior, we'll figure out the rest. If Mrs. Hill won't allow us to go into Washington with her, then we'll take our wagon and get there some other way."

Freeman said, "Sayre, let's do this one step at a time. No need to rush or worry. We'll need clear heads to find that horse and I'm afraid I won't be much help right now. We can hatch a plan together, but you'll have to carry it out."

"You're right. And you need to rest, too, so lie back down. Good night, Freeman. C'mon, Lady, we'll leave Gracie to guard Freeman and you can sleep next to me so both of us can stay warm."

The next morning the whole camp was bustling with excitement because in two days they would move across the Potomac. It was May 22, 1865. Freeman tried to help with chores, but he had to admit defeat in less than an hour and spent the rest of the day sitting outside the shed, basking in the warmth of the sun. Still, just seeing her friend healing this well after three anxious weeks was enough to buoy Sayre through the long day of work.

Since the night Freeman was shot, Sayre had begun a daily ritual of selecting a feather from her collection and slipping each into the band of her hat, like tiny amulets to ward off any setback or perhaps just bring a little extra luck. Other than these small decorative flourishes, she continued to dress as she had for the past several months. Right now it was unimportant to her whether people saw her as a boy or a girl. She was focused solely on two tasks: making sure Freeman regained his strength, and making sure the horses under her care recovered. The longstanding goal of finding Warrior was, at long last, within reach.

As Sayre passed Mrs. Hill's tent on her way to the hospital that evening, she heard cheerful voices coming from within. Remembering that Mrs. Hill had begun making lists of the men who wanted letters written or who needed Sayre to read to them to quiet their nerves or ease their pain, Sayre peeked around the corner.

"Excuse me, Mrs. Hill," she said softly, "I'm ready to read to the soldiers. Anyone in particular tonight?"

"Sayre, come in. This is Mother Bickerdyke, whom I've spoken about. Traveled with the army from Illinois to Atlanta working with the wounded men and then turned it over to me. She's here to be honored by President Johnson and General Sherman."

Sayre extended her hand to a woman dressed entirely in black, gray hair tucked neatly into a white cap. The elder woman's face was lively, her grip strong.

"Sayre, Mrs. Hill speaks highly of your work with our army, the men, the animals. I've even heard about the goat!" She glanced back at Mrs. Hill and they all three chuckled. "You've gotten quite a reputation in the Union Army. You must be very proud. We've been lucky to have you on our side." She paused, "Even for a short while."

"Thank you, ma'am," Sayre said. Fortified by this praise, she continued, "I was wondering if Freeman and I could accompany the men to Washington. We don't want to be in the parade, of course, but we would like to be there to see it. If we could travel with you to Washington and simply watch, we would be most grateful."

It was Mrs. Hill who responded. "We would be honored to have you continue with us into the capital. You, Freeman, and your band of rescues."

"Thank you," Sayre said and turned to leave.

"One more thing, Sayre," Mrs. Bickerdyke said. " Mrs. Hill and I will find something more appropriate for you to wear, something a little, shall we say, more feminine. We need strong women, and we want our newly reunited country to know that you, my dear girl, are a fine example of a strong woman. Before that, however, Mrs. Hill will speak with the wounded soldiers and the workers to let them know of your disguise. Will that be acceptable to you?"

Sayre shifted uncomfortably at the mention of her clothing. She responded in a soft voice, "I think that will be fine. Thank you."

Mrs. Hill smiled. "I agree wholeheartedly. You've faced great challenges and endured them with grace. One thing more, Sayre. With all of the Confederate soldiers coming by the camp, have you heard any news of your father?"

"No news at all. After the parade, we'll be heading back to Georgia to be there if he comes back." She caught herself and carefully spoke again. "I mean, when he comes back. Thank you for asking." She nodded at the two women to excuse herself.

"Sayre," Mrs. Hill called after her, "to answer your question, there's a Sergeant Mitchell who's been very sad today. He'll enjoy your company."

"Yes, ma'am," Sayre responded and hurried to the hospital to see Sergeant Mitchell.

CHAPTER 30

*S*herman's army moved toward Washington, not as a spit-and-shined band of warriors, but as a collage of battle-seasoned men and boys in a wide range of outfits. Some were barefoot, others wore mismatched pieces of clothing. Some had newly issued blue uniforms. Their appearance might be ragged, but every face was flushed with victory. It had been eight months since they'd left Atlanta, and now they were swarming into the outskirts of the capital, readying for the next day's parade to honor "Old Bill" Sherman. Nothing could dampen their spirits, not even the spring rains.

Freeman was determined to use his arm more each day, but the progress was slow. He'd begun the morning painstakingly helping Sayre and Parsy wash, clip,and curry three of the fifteen horses in their care, but then had to return to his cot to rest. Still, with help from Parsy's older children, every animal was soon gleaming and ready for the parade. Parsy even threw Lady and Gracie into the soap and water for good measure. Lady howled when the water touched her and Gracie bleated loudly while Sayre and the children roared with laughter at their antics. Even the tiny wagon from the farm was cleaned for the trip. Sayre scrubbed the boards and oiled Beauty's harnesses while Parsy worked on the wheels. Beauty, of course, did not escape the water. Sally saw to that.

Mrs. Hill had given Sayre a pair of brown pants that fit well and a light blue blouse that acknowledged her true figure. Sally had given her a great horned owl's feather, which Sayre tucked into the band of her hat to add a special touch for the occasion. Since the night Freeman had been shot, Sayre continued to layer her shirts for warmth and comfort while working with the animals.

Mrs. Hill, true to her word, had spoken to the wounded men in the hospital and the other workers at the camp about Sayre's disguise. Many of them had then told Sayre how proud they were of her for surviving the war in such a clever way and others had greeted her more warmly when she entered the hospital or was working in the stables. On some few occasions she heard whispered laughter when she passed by, but she ignored that and concentrated on her work or the thought of seeing Warrior.

Parsy, Sally, and the children had laughed and hugged her when she'd told them, wondering aloud how none of them had seen through her disguise.

Since Sayre and Freeman were not to be part of the parade itself, their plan was to follow the hospital wagons as voyeurs, assessing the situation, and looking for Warrior. Sayre knew her heart would always be with her beloved South, but for these last eight months she had lived with and been protected by the Northern army and good people like Mrs. Hill, Parsy, and Sally. She had entered the lives of fine men like Lt. Daniel, and had cared for scores of wounded Union horses. This celebration was a bittersweet time for her.

At the end of this long day, and with all of her tasks completed, Sayre walked to the pasture where Trace was munching hay with the other horses. His coat shone in the warming sun. Magic was nearby, his dark liver bay color shining rich against the background of trees, his head held high, his eyes now sparkling with life. Sayre sat down in the grass. As she looked at them, her eyes filled with tears. They, too, had fought hard, been scarred by the war and survived.

"Tomorrow," she said aloud, "tomorrow I may see Warrior, but if not tomorrow then someday soon. I know Freeman and I will find him. We've been cold, hungry, and dirty. We've seen destruction and sadness everywhere. We've rescued Moses, Magic, Gracie, and Lady, all with the hope of finding my horse. I can't believe we're still alive but we are. It's been a long journey and we still don't know the ending either with Warrior or with Papa."

She was startled from her reverie by a slight pressure on her left shoulder. Trace had left his hay and was standing next to her, his head lowered, his muzzle touching her. He had never done this before.

"How did you know my thoughts?" Sayre asked him.

Trace was silent.

Then she said, looking into those huge gentle eyes, "Thank you." She kissed his nose, breathing in his scent. "Lt. Daniel will be there, tomorrow, Trace. He'll be right there with you. Your name was the last thing he said before he died. He raised a very beautiful horse, you know that?"

She got up, patted Trace's neck, and walked to the barn. More work, some reading, and then sleep were waiting for her.

CHAPTER 31

"*S*ayre." Sally's voice awakened her. "It's time to get moving. The sun's about to come up. Parsy and I have the wagon ready. We need to feed the animals. They're raring to go. Must feel the excitement, I reckon. Parsy's helping Freeman dress. He's going to wear that new shirt I made for him."

"How did I miss all of this?" Sayre mumbled. "I thought I wouldn't sleep, but I must have dozed right off when I lay down on my cot, clothes and all. Give me a minute and I'll be ready."

Sayre hurriedly washed her face, put on her new clothes, and tucked the huge, speckled feather into her hatband. Outside, she paused to gaze at the wagon: Beauty was harnessed up to the old wagon she had pulled from Griswoldvillle. A garland of wildflowers was around her neck, a present from Sally and Parcy's children. Lady and Gracie were in their usual places, Lady on the seat, Gracie standing in the back; Trace and Magic were tied securely behind.

A tired-looking Freeman appeared and gingerly climbed onto the seat of the wagon. They were indeed ready to go as soon as Sally's family finished decorating the white mule that Parsy was to ride.

Although it was only 4 a.m., the camp was alive. Officers barked calls to the sergeants and the orders were passed down to the rank and file. Slowly, the huge war machine that

170

had cut through the underbelly of the Confederacy was assembling to head into the capital city. A sea of spectators, including President Johnson, General Grant and their revered commander, General Sherman, awaited them there.

Sayre settled into the wagon next to Freeman and took the reins into her hands as Parsy came up beside them. "Did you hear about yesterday when General Meade's forces were on parade?"

"Nope," Freeman replied, "My shoulder was achin' bad. I went to bed early. What happened?"

"Well, they say Meade's army was about eighty thousand strong, give or take. There were hundreds of pieces of artillery and his cavalry stretched for seven miles. Seems all of Washington was there to cheer for them. Sure hope they're still there 'cause we're gonna give them a real show. Course, we won't have as much spit and polish as they had, but we'll make up for it in spirit. Where will you and Sayre be?"

"I think we'll come last and sit and watch. That'll be just right for us," Freeman said.

"What do you mean?" exclaimed Parsy. "Ole Sherman's included everyone in the march: nurses, bummers, families who fled slavery, workers like me. You belong there too. He's even going to march the livestock he got down South, so your little herd of horses would fit right in."

"Thank you, Parsy," Sayre said, "But this victory is not ours. Still, we want to be there for you and all the others."

At that moment, somewhere a band struck up a march and the columns began to inch their way forward across the Potomac toward Pennsylvania Avenue. All around Sayre and Freeman, regiments began whooping, hollering, and cheering. Companies of men moved in from every direction. Parsy waved goodbye, then hurried to get astride his mule. Sally's wagon carrying the children fell in behind him.

Freeman and Sayre's plan was to get near Pennsylvania Avenue to see the parade and look for Warrior. They were, as they'd said, only spectators there to honor Parsy, his family, and the wounded men who rode in wagons ahead of them, some whom Sayre had grown to know and respect from reading to them or writing letters home. At one point, while waiting for more regiments to form, Sayre jumped from the wagon and ran to talk to some of the men in the medical wagons, knowing she wouldn't see them again once they were transferred to hospitals in the city.

One man said as Sayre leaned into the wagon to shake hands, "You look mighty fine today. That blue shirt suits you."

"Thank you," she answered. "It seems blue's the color of victory today. You stay well, Sergeant Poole. Get back to Illinois safely. I know your family's waiting for you."

"Sure are," he said. "I hope they'll welcome a one-armed father."

"No doubt about it," she answered with a smile. "I sure will be glad to welcome back my papa, whatever happened to him." She had to turn away quickly to master a sudden rush of emotion. Knowing that her father, wherever he might be, would not be enjoying a parade, Sayre took a deep breath and continued on her rounds, with a special word for each soldier she knew.

When she returned to the wagon, she settled in and held Lady close. Saying good-bye to these brave men was difficult, more difficult than she had imagined. Gracie bleated and placed her chin on top of Sayre's head, one of her favorite positions when unnerved by new surroundings. Sayre had put a rope around the goat's neck and she held it now to keep her from leaping into the crowd.

Sayre turned to Freeman, laughing. "I'm glad we're not going to be part of the parade. Actually we look like part of a traveling show, a one-eyed mule, a dog, a goat and two horses. What a spectacle we are!"

Freeman smiled and looked around the wagon. "Yes," he said. "I think you're right."

Sayre slowly guided Beauty to the top of a hill and pulled her to a halt. From this vantage point, there was a clear view down the famous avenue. Both Freeman and Sayre blinked in amazement.

Before them sprawled Pennsylvania Avenue- broad, beautiful, but dusty in the morning light. Throngs of people were everywhere: on the street, on balconies, and atop roofs. It seemed that everyone had a banner, a flag, flowers or wreaths, many in red, white, or blue. The sound of their exultant cheers was almost deafening.

General Sherman was at the head of the ragtag band that had ended the war. The way he rode his favorite horse, Lexington, showed he was immensely proud of the way his men had fought, suffered valiantly, and finally prevailed. The war, which had so nearly dissolved the Union, was over.

Each unit began its descent into the crowds. Right behind Sherman, Kilpatrick's Cavalry came riding stirrup to stirrup on the most stunning horses in the parade. Each animal's coat shone, each mane was clipped to the crest, and every piece of tack was polished to perfection. Sayre, without thinking, leapt up on the wagon seat, her eyes searching for one head, the brilliant chestnut color, a mane and tail glowing in the sun.

Suddenly the columns halted, the cheers quieted, and the band stopped playing. President Johnson spoke to the crowd and to the soldiers as General Sherman paused and dismounted before the reviewing stand. All the dignitaries stood with their hats in their hands, a show of respect for the huge mass of soldiers arrayed before them and for their stalwart commander.

To Sayre and Freeman, the president's voice was a distant murmur, but Sayre wasn't listening. Her eyes moved intently from horse to horse, searching the cavalry that stood in perfect formation near the reviewing stand. Then she saw a shape she recognized, a flank, a tail flecked with sunlight. She jumped to the ground and bolted from the wagon.

Freeman shouted, "Sayre! Stop! Not now!"

But she didn't pause. She broke into a run. All she could see was Warrior- huge, powerful, and alive. Nothing was around her. She was in the pasture in Georgia where her horse grazed. She was running to get him, to gallop up the hillside, to feel the cool air whipping through her hair, his powerful muscles beneath her. And there was her father in the field, her mother hanging clothes on the line. Now, she whistled his call, the little song he knew was his summons, but this Warrior stood motionless, dutiful to his regimental rider.

Undeterred, Sayre ran faster. Her hat flew from her head. She whistled the notes again, dashing past more wagons and the soldiers in front of them. On the third whistle, Warrior turned, breaking from his position. With a startled look, his rider tried to pull the horse back into the line. Sayre whistled a fourth time and Warrior reared, whinnied and wheeled. The officer hastily dismounted, and threw the reins over the horse's head, preparing to walk him to the side and settle him down, but Warrior turned swiftly, deftly, and broke away. His walk was high, regal, the walk of a Saddle-bred in true form. The reins swung from side to side as he began to trot, then canter toward Sayre.

The stunned crowd, dignitaries and soldiers watched in silence as the horse and girl rushed toward each other. Sayre heard a cheer from the hospital wagons behind her, but all she could see was Warrior, her Warrior! She stopped and whispered his name, and he slowed, then walked to her. She threw her arms around his neck and buried her head into his chest to inhale his scent once more.

CHAPTER 32

A voice penetrated her reverie. "I call him Blade. He's a magnificent horse."

Sayre, startled, looked up to see Captain Henry. His gray eyes were twinkling and a slight smile parted his lips. Sayre had forgotten how handsome he was, and now she felt exposed and, for once, very timid.

"His name is Southern Warrior," she said softly. "I call him Warrior, for short. He was stolen from me after you rode by my farm near Griswoldville, Georgia, but I doubt that you remember."

It was as if her breath ran out as she looked around and realized that neither the parade nor President Johnson and General Grant were now the focus of this crowd. Everyone, whether military or civilian, was silently watching her. She lifted Warrior's reins and handed them to Captain Henry.

"Here," she said, "please ride him during the parade. You've both fought hard, and I can see how well you've treated him. I guess I'm not surprised, since he does have a way of winning hearts."

The captain's brow furrowed. He, too, was aware of the attention from his men and his superiors.

"Could I meet you after the parade is over?" Sayre asked.

"That's a fair offer. I'll look for you where the parade ends on Pennsylvania Avenue, "Captain Henry said as he took the reins and mounted Warrior and turned the horse back toward his spot in the cavalry configuration.

Sayre turned and walked back to Freeman. Nothing seemed real now. She picked up her hat along the way and shoved it onto her head. Somehow, Freeman had managed to position the wagon under a tree away from the throngs still waiting to deploy into the parade. Sayre climbed aboard. Lady cuddled next to her, and Gracie again put her head on top of Sayre's. Freeman sat quietly, holding the reins in his lap.

He turned to her. "How 'bout we just sit here and clap for Parsy and his family when they go by, and for all the other men we know. I've had about as much excitement as I can stand today."

Sayre's heart was pounding so hard she thought everyone could hear it. She smiled at Freeman, then moved to the back of the wagon to stand and cheer as their friends rolled past to savor the victory and the day that was theirs.

When the parade was over, Parsy rode back to where Sayre and Freeman waited. "Mighty good view from here," he said as he slid to the ground. "Sayre, I'm guessing that horse is yours. Freeman told me why he was fighting for the Union. I bet that horse's got plenty of good stories to tell. Oh," he laughed, "you should have seen ol' Billy Sherman's face when that animal broke rank! But then he smiled when he saw you comin' down the road. Shows the man has a sense of humor."

"Yes, that's my horse. His name is Southern Warrior and he was stolen from me. I couldn't have found him without Freeman or, for that matter, all of you."

Freeman chuckled and shook his head. "Parsy, could we ask one more favor? Could you go back to where the stable tack boxes are and fetch a bridle, reins,pad, and saddle? We're going to meet the captain and we may do a little exchanging."

"I'd be proud to. Then I think I'll tag along to see the end of all this."

Sayre beamed at him. "Thank you. That would be wonderful. We would never have made it without you helping us find a spot in the Union Army, of all places. We'll wait right here."

Soon, Parsy returned with the tack and helped Sayre put it on Trace. She looped the reins over the horse's head and tied him to the wagon with a rope, then sat down beside Freeman. Parsy rode beside the wagon.

Freeman guided Beauty to a side street that ran parallel to Pennsylvania Avenue and on to the spot where the parade ended. The regiments were scattering in every direction. Each would be billeted around the city to await money, clothes, and orders. The wounded were to be parceled out to the various hospital units that had been set up in or near the city. The country was beginning its long march back to unity.

Freeman and Sayre turned onto the bottom of Pennsylvania Avenue and stopped to look for Captain Henry and Warrior. The sounds of the festivities ebbed and flowed around them. No one spoke. Sayre raised her head with the sound of each horse coming near. Hours later the streets finally cleared as the revelers either went home or moved their partying to other sections of the city.

As the daylight faded into dusk, Sayre climbed down from the wagon and walked a short distance, took off her hat, and held it in her hand still watching the street for any sign of the captain and her beloved horse. Finally she said, "Well, Freeman, either the captain has been detained with urgent business, or he has no intention of returning Warrior to me. Let's head back to camp and decide what we're going to do. Warrior's here. The captain's here. We just have to find them."

Freeman sighed. When he spoke, he sounded tired. "Times get harder and harder, I'm afraid, Sayre. Folks work hard, put their heart into something and rely on other folks to do the right thing. When they disappoint us, it hurts pretty bad. You're right, though. For now let's head back, check on the horses, and put our heads together."

Chores completed, Sayre led Trace to the makeshift corral and turned him and Gracie lose. She pulled herself up to the top of the fence surrounding it and sat there watching the pair enjoy their freedom. Freeman was resting after the long day, and she didn't want to disturb him. Warrior's face kept appearing before her, and she relived over and over again the moment when she had actually touched him today. She had come so close, and now another obstacle had surfaced. She was so very tired.

"Trace," she called. "Come here, beautiful man. Let me rub your face."

The horse's ears moved in her direction, he whinnied softly, and moved toward Sayre in a gentle canter, his long, dark mane dancing from side to side. He came to a halt near her and his eyes met hers. She gently stroked his head as she breathed in his scent. "He was so close to me today, Trace," she whispered. "So very close."

She was so engrossed in her thoughts that she didn't hear the rustle of skirts behind her until Mrs. Bickerdyke asked, "Is that the horse you have been looking for? I've been anxious to see him after learning your story."

Sayre turned, realized who it was, and slid quickly down to the ground.

"No, ma'am. I'm afraid it's not. This is Trace, Lt. Daniel's horse. They were both badly wounded. Lt. Daniel died, but Freeman and I were able to save his horse. I'm afraid Warrior is still missing."

"What do you mean?' asked Mrs. Bickerdyke.

"Well, Captain Henry was supposed to meet us after the parade broke up, but Freeman, Parsy and I waited all day and he never came."

"What will you do now?" the older woman asked.

"You know I have no idea," Sayre said. "I guess we begin our search all over again, only this time we'll concentrate on a city and not three states. Right now all I can think of just being so close to Warrior today, and how wonderful it was. I've always had a plan before. Now I don't. But I won't give up!"

"I'm sorry, Sayre," Mrs. Bickerdyke said. "I was hoping to see your Southern Warrior. Now I have to go back to the mounds of paperwork I have to finish in order to get these brave men into the proper facilities. Good night."

Sayre extended her hand and Mrs. Bickerdyke shook it warmly. "Thank you, ma'am, for all you've done for us. Freeman and I will think of something, I know. It's just a small setback, I hope."

After Mrs. Bickerdyke left, Sayre walked back to the stable and sat down next to Magic's stall. Freeman was fast asleep. As always, Lady was curled up on the floor near his cot, but when Sayre came in she got up and sat down beside her, her head in her lap. "Today was a good day," Sayre whispered to the big dog. "I'll just sit here for a while with you. I think going to my little room would be very lonely right now."

CHAPTER 33

S ayre and Freeman were up early the next day. Sayre did most of the morning chores because Freeman went to talk with Parsy to see if he had any connections in the army to find out where Kilpatrick's cavalry was billeted. Sayre was changing the dressing on one of the horse's wounds when Freeman returned.

"Well, Sayre," he said. "Parsy's gonna ask around and we'll go from there. That's about it for now. We're not sure how we can make a captain in the U.S. Army surrender a horse, but that'll come after findin' 'im. Anyway, we've –"

"Pardon me," a voice said, "but I have some news."

Sayre and Freeman turned to see Mrs. Bickerdyke, dressed in her traditional black dress and white cap, a starched white collar surrounding her rather plump face. "Sayre, your horse will be here in a few minutes. Your Captain Henry located us." With that she turned and walked out of the stable, a stunned Sayre and Freeman following. When they reached the entrance to the camp, Captain Henry, astride Warrior, was coming over the hill. Sayre stood transfixed as the pair stopped in front of her and the captain dismounted.

Mrs. Bickerdyke went to the captain and introduced herself, then continued, turning to Sayre. "Captain Henry sent his orderly to me this morning with news that he wanted to talk with you. I'm very impressed, captain, very impressed. I will now leave the three of you to discuss your plans for Southern Warrior." A smile then lit up her face. "He's a beautiful animal. I would have searched for him also, Sayre"

For a brief moment no one spoke. Then Freeman said, "Captain Henry, sir, Sayre and I are actually proposing a trade. Lieutenant Daniel's horse, Trace, is in the corral over there. He came in hurt pretty bad the day the lieutenant died, but now Trace is fit for duty again. Had a lot of love and special attention from us both. He's a fine mount."

Captain Henry cleared his throat, and, then spoke, his voice firm but low. "That sounds like a fair deal to me. It wouldn't have yesterday, but after a sleepless night of thinking, I know where Warrior belongs. It took a little doing to find out who you were and to connect you to Mrs. Bickerdyke, but then the pieces fell into place. My orders are to take my brigade to Georgia to do a bit of mopping up. The roads are rough and dangerous. I would be pleased if you would join the other civilians we're escorting south. If you would be so good to stay in Washington for a few days, I'll let you know when my men will be ready to leave. Perhaps you could stay near Mrs. Bickerdyke while she transfers the wounded men to hospitals in the area. That will make it easy for me to find you."

Then Captain Henry turned to Warrior. "Don't worry. I'll see that you get back to Georgia, old man. You and I have had a good ride!" Then he handed Sayre the reins.

Sayre gripped them tightly. "Thank you," she said. "Thank you from all of us."

"And now, Captain," Freeman began. "If you'll get your saddle and blanket off Warrior, we'll find Trace and I'll saddle him up for ya."

When they had gone, Sayre took a few steps forward and cradled Warrior's powerful head in her arms. She leaned her head against his muscled neck and turned to lead him to the stable. She had only taken a step when, from the corner of her eye, she saw a flash of red sparkling in the grass. She dropped the reins, knelt down, moved a few leaves and picked up the cardinal's feather. It felt warm in her hand.

"Thank you, papa," she said. Then she looked up at Warrior towering above her, his face very near hers. She closed her eyes and whispered, "Welcome back, Southern Warrior. Finally we're heading home."

#

CPSIA information can be obtained
at www.ICGtesting.com
Printed in the USA
FFOW02n0918240214
3783FF

9 781457 525230